I Knew It in the Bath

I Knew It in the Bath

Linda Flynn

Bridge House

British Library Cataloguing in Publication Data
A Record of this Publication is available from the British
Library

ISBN 978-1-914199-28-8

This edition published 2022 by Bridge House Publishing
Manchester, England

In memory of Mum and Dad

"Those who find beauty in all of nature will find themselves at one with the secrets of life itself."
L. Wolfe Gilbert

Contents

Introduction

The bath tub is the place where dreams and possibilities flow as easily as the tap water – if only they would go to plan.

I Knew it in the Bath is a collection of short stories which show that no matter how we expect events to unfold, life has a way of confounding us.

What will a woman do to save her friend? Do we really know when we're being watched? Why did Dora throw the iron through the window? What's the best way to take revenge on a cheating partner?

Settle back to read through these humorous, sinister and thought-provoking stories, but try not to drop your book in the bath!

Climbing Rainbows

"Reality leaves a lot to the imagination."

John Lennon

No-one knew why Dora threw the iron through the window.

Decent, dreamy Dora, in her smudge grey clothes, with her pale face that hardly raised a smile, much less flung an iron.

The neighbours could not have been more shocked if a meteorite had landed in their front garden. Their friend Greg laughed that she was stressed, but his wife Tamsin whispered that she was going through The Change. Her husband complained about the cost of the pane and Dora hid the cost of her pain.

The act of extreme ironing requires significant manual dexterity, alongside the thrill of coping with the treacherous mountain terrain. Dora has completed the shirt collar with a flourish and is in the act of abseiling down, when the cuffs become more problematic. A momentary loss of concentration results in the iron sliding from her grasp as it follows a curved trajectory down the mountain side.

Next door but one looked at Dora askance. He had once given her a disparaging smirk and informed her that with her lack of presence she would make an excellent spy. Dora found the proposed insult surprisingly appealing and practised melting into shadows, or moulding herself into the corners of rooms, where she would glean all kinds of interesting snippets.

It was when she was laying the table for the cricket tea that she heard Greg call out to one of his team, "Watch out, big head Ed's coming out to bowl!" The corner of her mouth gave the smallest upward turn as she chopped chunks of cheese.

In a quiet spot by the side of the pavilion, Dora kicked open her deckchair. She sighed, for her challenge now was to feign interest in the game.

The secret of white-water rafting is to gain maximum momentum whilst steering between rocks without overturning the craft. With buttocks clenched firmly on the inflatable seat, Dora hooks one foot under the cross tube and the other braced firmly on the floor. Her arms reach out as she paddles forward, before leaning across and plunging the raft away from hazards.

Later it was assumed that Dora had become too engrossed in Ed's bowling. She was found suspended upside down in her deckchair with her legs poking up in the air, just like one of her sausages on sticks.

To celebrate and prolong his victory, Ed made the benevolent gesture of inviting Greg from the opposing team, with his wife Tamsin to dinner. Dora cooked and Ed opened the wine.

The game was replayed in slow motion, until finally Dora could remove the plates.

"Don't worry, Dora will do the dishes!" called out Ed, flashing a goofy grin. "After all, she's the one who made most of them dirty." Tamsin glanced at the stacked pile of crockery and smiled a faint apology as she slid out of the kitchen.

Dora looked too, at her husband, then at the congealed fat slowly sliding off the cooking tray, before sweeping it up and piling it clattering into the sink. She kicked the door shut on the laughter and the murmur of conversation.

For Dora is a plate spinner and her act requires the deepest concentration. Already she has two plates turning on the draining board, running in rivulets of gravy. She is adding a third, a fourth; can she really keep this going? Dora now has six plates spinning on the side, whilst

11

juggling three more in the air, all of this accompanied to the tune of the Sabre Dance.

There was a momentary lapse in conversation when a crash was heard in the kitchen, but no-one left their seat.

The music in Dora's head changes to Zorba the Greek.

The following morning a slight misunderstanding arose. Dora was stripping the duvet cover to go into the laundry basket. Unfortunately, Ed was still asleep in bed.

Dora Grey scarcely notices, for she is bracing herself to participate in the extreme sport of Blobbing. First she must climb to the highest point, before plunging herself at speed on to the giant air bag, which has someone waiting at the other end to be bounced off. She knows that the higher and heavier her jump, the greater that person will lift off. Let the Blobbing battle begin!

The mattress was replaced fairly quickly, but Ed took a little longer.

———————

Published in *Transformations,* December 2020 as one of the winning entries in the Waterloo Festival.

Unseen Eyes

"The resolution to avoid an evil is seldom framed till the evil is so far advanced as to make avoidance impossible."

Thomas Hardy

You always know when you are being watched. There's that sense of a tingling in your spine, a boring into your back, or an awareness that every detail is being observed. And all without you turning around.

Most of the time you would brush it away, forgotten, like the litter blowing across the platform. At other times you might freeze, knowing that you are almost alone, as you try to focus on the peeling posters. The train rushes in like an indrawn breath and you leap on.

You know it's not unusual, it happens to everyone, so why is it troubling you today?

A quick glance around the carriage, without making any eye contact, assures you that everything is normal: faces buried in newspapers, books or phones, a pale pensive man twisting some interview notes in his lap, a ginger haired girl impatiently kicking her legs against the seat, figures stood at the poles turned away from each other. Then the deep, dark blur of the tunnel as the windows gleamed back dull reflections. So why is your heart beating a little faster?

You rub your eyes; you hadn't slept well last night, haunted by the shadowy outline by the bush outside your bedroom window.

The train seems to wait ages at the station. It's hard not to drum your fingers as passengers heave on and off. An obstruction in the doors. At last it surges forward and those standing sway backwards.

You scan the new faces, clenching your hands which are now clammy with dread.

You see a black jacket weaving through the passengers. It's the same as a thousand other black jackets seen on the underground, but there's something in the straightness of the back, an alertness, and the air around you feels suffocating.

Of course neighbours meet each other all the time: chance encounters buying a pint of milk, collecting a newspaper, walking a dog. But still, not all the time, not the exact same routine.

You should have taken a taxi. Too late to think of that now.

The hooded mac helps. Not your usual raincoat. You don't even like it much, but bland beige blends in.

The train screeches to the penultimate stop before you must disembark. Your heart is hammering. You glance down at your shoes. Not ideal for walking.

You hold your breath and in your head begin counting the three seconds it will take for the doors to fully close. Then you leap out at one, forcibly parting people as you sprint on to the platform.

A hurried glance behind; then breathe. You flit into the gap between commuters, knowing the space will close as people jostle forward.

Before you reach the escalator you slip off your coat, scrunch it into a ball and shove it into your bag. Black clothes. Good.

Your heart is thumping but you must take the escalator calmly, without drawing attention to yourself; so you ease in front of a bulky man and remain motionless, steadying your pulse.

The crowd on the pavement outside has thinned, so you slip inside a busy shop, slide past customers and out of a side door. It's all time lost and you will be late for work; if only you had left slightly earlier today.

There's the reassuring rumble of traffic and once more you are swallowed up by a group of pedestrians. You keep pace with them; there's safety in numbers. Everyday conversations flitter around you, dull and reassuring, people going about their every-day lives.

You try to resist turning your head around, checking, watching. With an effort of will you face mainly forwards, throwing the occasional glance at reflections in shop windows. There's nothing unusual and you are nearly there.

As you approach the main door to your office your knees feel weak with relief and you long to sit down.

Instinct makes you twist your head slightly towards the café window opposite. Then you see him. He gives a half smile and seems to raise his coffee cup in greeting.

He was there before you; he already knew where you worked.

You thought you had noticed when you were being watched, but you hadn't, not really. Another detail had been given away, another piece of the jig-saw puzzle that formed your life, another fact gleaned from following; making you easier to stalk.

Published in *Resolutions*, December 2021, Bridge House.

An immersive theatre version of the story was also published in *The Script Challenge* by Bridge House Publishing.

"There's Rosemary, That's for Remembrance."
William Shakespeare, Hamlet

"A wise woman knows how to summon her courage and do what is right, rather than what is easy."

Suze Orman

"To see a candle's light one must take it into a dark place."

Ursula Le Guin

Doctor Archibald Tobias was found at noon, lying as still as a tomb.

There are gossips in every village and Lydney was no exception. Some claimed that mandrake roots had been boiled in his stew, a few loudly proclaimed it was witchcraft, but the softer whispers said that he had sampled some of his own medicine.

He had considered himself to be a master of his profession, trained by the best medical men in the country, at Cambridge University. His expertise earned him the right to visit the wealthiest patients around Gloucestershire, where he would bowl up in his new pony and gig. Many a wealthy land owner would sigh with relief, to see him strut through their gate with his chest out and his leather bag bulging with the latest learning. He would leave only a bill of his charges behind, with perhaps a jar of leeches for blood-letting and instructions to be presented to the apothecary for their medicines.

Whilst on his rounds he would often notice Rosemary, the village wise-woman, wending her way from one hovel to another, administering her home-spun, primitive herbal cures and he would smile.

She never returned his greetings, just narrowed her cat-like green eyes, and with a twist of her tawny head would slip off into the woodland. He noted that she seemed to glide through nature without disturbing it. Even the birds and deer did not seem to take off in flight. This was an uncommon woman.

He thought again of the haughty way she held herself upright and her disdainful gaze, as though she was the one who was high born, and found himself bristling. He whipped his pony harder than he intended, so with an abrupt wrench his trap jerked forward and he clung to the sides to steady himself.

Rosemary weaved her way through the brooding willows that found themselves alongside the meandering river, skirting its dark green glass edges, before it opened up into fields swathed with sunlit grass.

She had prepared a potion laced with a little belladonna to help with Mary's birth pains and her baby's passage into the world. Then she used a mixture of lavender and mandragora to help with John's death pains, the sleep assisting his passage into the next world.

She sauntered towards the village, gathering herbs in her basket, ready to give to Bess to dry out later in her cottage. They would be pummelled into potions and ointments.

As she approached the grey stone cross, where three mud tracks converged, she felt a sense of trepidation. Shadows were flung across the monument from the sprawled branches of the old oak, which were flailing in all directions. Shrill cries and raucous shouts resounded, shaking the air. She ran forward, raising her arms, as her hair slipped around her like fire. The gathering groups parted to allow her through.

In the centre of the mounted stone blocks she observed Ann, with her face flushed and her chin raised. On either side of her, with legs parted were Joshua and Tom, glaring at each other.

Rosemary nodded, she knew this pot had been about to boil.

First she beckoned Tom towards her. With defiant eyes he stepped forward. As she walked with him away from the others, she placed her arm over his. "Tom, you are to leave at daybreak, without a word to anyone. Follow the river's path westward and take yourself into one of the nearby villages. Only return when the sun has set over the river nine times, and not before. Then and only then, you should meet Ann by the Mill Bridge and present her with the most beautiful stone that you find on your travels."

To Joshua she smiled and said, "Ann is like that oak tree; her roots grow deep, solid and unmoving. You are more like the rushing brook beneath, ever restless, never still. Take your trade eastward in the direction of this river and do not return until the moon has waxed and waned a full nine times. When it has done so, you will have found the brightest sun and Ann will be but a shadow."

Rosemary ignored Ann's mutinous face as she walked her away from the on-lookers. She simply pointed to the sky and said, "Tonight look to the stars winking in the sky. Tom is your bright and constant North Star, giving you direction.

"Joshua is but a shooting star in August, shining all the more brightly for burning himself out."

Tobias watched her body wind its way through a field of wheat in a silent, smooth, sinuous movement. He noticed the way that the coarse fabric of her dress clung to her soft, white body, whilst her hair blazed out behind her in a wild, wanton display.

He saw her pause, tilting her head slightly, as a deer does when it scents danger.

As swift as the breeze she slipped off in a different

direction, leaving only the nodding corn sheaves behind her.

There it came again, that pulsing heat, the sense of being observed. She scanned the clumps of trees with her sharp green eyes.

A snap of a twig and a rustling of wings drew her to a dark hunched shape flattened to a tree trunk.

It was not far to the farm cottage from the field, but she still had to traverse the stream that ran through the copse. Her shallow breathing caught in her throat. To break free, she would either need to go closer and then run; or she could flee in the opposite direction.

In a heartbeat she swung around and cut diagonally across the corn, feeling the blades scrape her legs. She would not turn around.

Tobias' cheeks burned. He had been turned away from the Great House; they no longer required his ministrations.

His eyes bulged as he stared into the serving girl's sparrow-like face. Old George's fever had worsened in the night, in spite of all of his blood-letting.

By morning they had brought in Rosemary with her basket of herbs, who had undone all of his good work by removing the leeches, throwing open the shutters and banking the fire.

They had chosen superstitious folklore over his wealth of learning from the most erudite men in the country.

After the Great House, Rosemary rushed to the farmhouse where she administered a blend of sage, lavender and marjoram along Nan's brow to ease her headache.

She gave some rosemary for her stomach pains and burnt the rest to clear the air. She patted Nan's hand. "Pay no heed to scandalmongers, for they have no more substance than if you look at your visage in the river, where ripples distort your image."

Tobias noticed that whilst Rosemary did not charge for her dispensations, she did not go short. For even though her cottage lay on the outskirts of the village, every day fresh goods were left on the step. He shook his head at the eggs, milk and a bolt of cloth waiting to be brought inside. Her needs were always met.

Inside Bess was drying herbs across the rafters, preparing lotions, grinding up plants and boiling potions in a rounded iron pot.

He had two assistants of his own now, scavenged from Cambridge: wiry young labourers with crooked smiles, eager to earn some money. As Rosemary appeared, hastening towards her home, he pressed a coin into each of their clammy hands. With alacrity they rushed to block her path, ogling her as they did so.

Rosemary did not halt her pace, keeping her strides long and purposeful. As she drew level she said, "The wind makes a cruel and fickle task master. It blusters and moans with a great show of strength as it fells the mighty elm."

Her dark green eyes looked straight into their faces. "But it can quickly change direction."

They stepped aside.

Often in the dark of the moon, when Rosemary lit a tallow with its flickering flame distorting shadows around her cottage, she would get a sense of a brooding ill-boding outside. Amidst the bats flitting and the swoop of a barn owl, she would see the bushes shudder, or the gate swing open, or a dark mound lying on the ground that had not been there before.

In the pool of pulsing light, she would lie on her straw pallet with taut muscles, listening to the foxes barking and alert for any strange sounds.

Tobias stood behind the hay rick watching her water divining. The farmer wanted to know the source of the underground spring. She stood with a hazel twig in each hand, walking backwards and forwards, an absent expression on her face. Suddenly the twigs turned in towards each other and she stood motionless as the farmer pointed towards the spot.

Only the devil could be part of such sorcery.

Hunched inside Martha's hovel, she observed her weary movements. "I have prepared a chamomile tincture to help with your malady of the mind," Rosemary offered, as she crouched opposite, so that their knees were nearly touching.

"We must follow the course of the river, wherever it takes us, for that is our fate. Sometimes it twists and winds with firm, steep banks through sunny, open pastures, or clear bubbling brooks. But it also becomes deep, dark and dank, where the water hardly seems to flow. Remember that these are the places where the biggest fish grow."

She touched Martha's arm and left the ointment.

The air became stifling and still; Rosemary struggled to breathe. Her legs felt heavy as she stumbled towards her cottage. "Bess! I must take my leave, you must go!"

"No! Why?" Bess covered her face with her hands.

Rosemary slid some of her tools onto a shelf up the chimney. The herbs and potions she pushed into a roof cavity. "Three witnesses claim that they saw me casting love spells by the stone cross. I am also going to be charged with practising sorcery amongst nature, locating hidden stones with mystical qualities and dispensing magical potions in Lydney village."

Bess recalled the day in her childhood when she had been forced to watch the ducking and drowning of a witch in the deepest part of the river. She froze in horror.

Rosemary led her to the door frame and as she passed through the threshold bestowed upon Bess a stealth blessing to help her remain unobserved:

"Be as still as the waiting heron,
As silent as the owl in flight,
As watchful as the eagle's eye,
And hidden in the darkest night."

Rosemary's body was hanged from the great oak tree. For three nights they left it there for the carrion to feed upon. On the night of a full moon it was cut down and burned. The blackened remains crumbled into the scarred, scorched earth.

Summoned to Doctor Archibald Tobias' white washed room, Bess clenched and unclenched her skirts. His face was clammy and as white as marble, as vice-like cramps clenched his stomach.

"If the doctor from the next parish cannot help you, with his bad blood-letting, then I don't know what I can do. My mistress died before I had time to learn her craft."

His pale eyes darted around the room. "What is that which lies on my window sill?" he rasped.

Bess slid over and presented the dark green stalk with purple heart-shaped petals. "It is nought but a stem of rosemary."

By noon, Doctor Archibald Tobias was found dead, crushing a sprig of rosemary between his fingers.

Published in *Mulling it Over*, November 2020, Bridge House.

Shouting in a Sandstorm

"They may forget what you said – but they will never forget how you made them feel."

Carl W. Buehner

My mother sits in the same chair, watching the scene unfold before her. It begins as a murky grey day in which the sky and sea seem to merge. Gradually the tide retreats, laying the beach bare for the dramas to be enacted upon it. The sun spot lights the ridged sand amid cries of laughter, barking dogs and shrieks of seagulls. Colours and shapes flap in and out of her vision, as she sits hunched in a fluffy pink cardigan, enclosed in her own fuzzy world.

It began with a bag. Like so many insignificant things, it gained importance with memory; mine that is, not hers. She never forgot her handbag when she went to the shops, yet that day she left it lying limply in the porch.

I scooped it up and ran after her, knowing that something was wrong, but not understanding how events would unfold. My breath caught in the freshening wind. I found her staring in the newsagent's window with a frown on her face. Her hand flew to her mouth as I passed her bag over. She recovered quickly with a smile and we brushed the moment over. It was a snapshot of the life that was to come; one we wanted to delete.

Our hair flapped around our faces as we walked back along the beach, welcoming the distraction of the stinging wind. Whirlwinds of sand were whipped up and thrashed against our legs. Still we trudged on with our heads bowed, unable to see where we were walking. Billowing clouds reared up like saffron waves. We tried to call out to each other, but our words were whisked up into the air and somersaulted away, filling our mouths with gritty sand.

After a few minutes the storm eased enough for us to raise our heads and look around, before heading towards the damper sand. There our feet sank into a soggy mush, oozing into puddles, before our prints were obliterated.

I check that my mother is not too warm by the window, but her hand flaps me away. A bad day. Her cool control has been loosened like a band that has lost its elasticity. Speech which had once flowed freely drizzled through her mind.

At first the words clustered together in sticky clumps. Helplessly I watched her wrestle for them: squinting her eyes, as they jumbled through her once brilliant brain, erupting in a tangle or twisting, turning, tumbling out of view.

Friends fled in tears, unable to confront her infirmity and their own frailty. Her chest squeezed with their anguish.

At times she would have a piercing flash of realisation that lost words were more easily hidden in silence.

I place a photo album on her lap, her past captured as she stood up straight in a suit, clutching a briefcase. Her eyes look straight at the camera, full of confidence for the future. Now her sharp edges have been sanded down. When I look at my mother, I search to see her in this sweet, gentle stranger.

I turn the pages of her recorded life. Clouds clear across her face as she gives a glimmer of recognition. She points. Just for a moment, laughter lifts her like a lark, singing, soaring higher into the sky. Then the bars crash down and the bird is caged once more.

Her eyes squeeze shut, her hand pummels the air. She is screaming inside.

My mother tries to speak but the words keep sliding off her tongue, slipping away like ice cubes.

Her gaze becomes wistful, far away. I wrap a shawl around her shoulders although she does not stir. Outside the window the clouds bunch together, the sun retreats. The tide pours in, clearing the beach, wiping away all trace of what has been.

Published in *Transformations*, December 2020, an anthology of winning stories from the Waterloo Festival.

The Litter in Glitter

"People are like stained-glass windows. They sparkle and shine when the sun is out, but when the darkness sets in, their true beauty is revealed only if there is a light from within."

Elisabeth Kubler-Ross

"The scale of the mess we leave behind is proportionate to the level of respect we have for others."

Stewart Stafford

A flicker of light glinted through brooding grey clouds as Rose pulled the rumbling bins behind her. The park. A perfect start to her day, somewhere peaceful, with only the stirring of bird song.

She speared up the litter, careful to straighten her back to avoid a stooping ache.

A bin spewed out some half eaten sandwiches, broken pieces of blue plastic, a baby's dummy and some broken glass. Lucky that she had found this litter before a child had stepped in it, or fatally a puppy had run off with a small object in its mouth.

Rose gazed upwards through the web of branches of an old oak tree and pulled down a flapping plastic bag.

The yellowing sky opened its spot light on the park as it slowly awakened. A blackbird hopped upon a twig, the gate creaked open and a swish of bike tyres sped along the path.

Bruised clouds bunched together again as she completed her circuit. She neared the groaning traffic, the air became clogged with fumes and her bins filled quickly. After the first drop off point she had to cover both sides of the High Street. In her regulation fluorescent yellow jacket and grey

26

waterproof trousers with the luminous stripe, she felt strangely anonymous, sure that people would look through her. Even so, she felt a flutter of fear at recognition.

In the take-away quarters, she scraped up some old rice, dog's mess and worse, some chewing gum which would need to be blasted off the pavement. Shattered pieces of glass lay in pools, winking in the remaining rays of the sun.

Rose looked at the purple clouds and pulled up her hood. Leaflets fluttered in the rising breeze and she struggled to capture them. One escaped and slumped soggily in an oily puddle. She paused when she saw the crimson heading of "St Benedict's Art College". In her gloved hand she read, "On 1st April at 19.00 talented Art students will be holding an Art Presentation with a difference, all of the exhibits will be demonstrated on stage to an audience, instead of at a roam around exhibition. The local media and companies have been invited." Details of obtaining tickets followed as Rose pummelled the limp leaflet into her glove.

Once again she recalled how her fingers had been poised to knock at the studio door. Her mind was sparking with ideas for the exhibition and she longed to share them.

Her hand dropped to her side. Through the rectangular grids of the safety glass she saw him with his back to her, his arm around an animated woman.

Her soul sunk. She stood transfixed. The woman gave a tinkling laugh and shook her auburn hair as they both turned to look towards the door way.

Rose turned and ran, her breath coming in shuddering gasps. She had to escape the truth, to put some distance between her and them.

In the past she had not minded the age difference, or that he was her lecturer; she had been flattered. Of all the students, he had noticed her, nurtured her talent, shown her

27

that she was someone special. She had glowed in his spotlight.

Rose's eyes hazed over when she reached the railway bridge. All that she had left now was her pride. The canvases that he had praised, the compositions that he had encouraged, all were left behind. She never wanted to see them again.

Now she felt as though she lived in a vacuum, without colour or brightness, murky grey.

Rose shuffled forward and elbowed a loose strand of hair out of her eyes as the first drops of rain fell. She tried to tug her hood further over her head as pedestrians scurried past, registering her presence no more than the pigeons at her feet.

Under a shop's canopy she scooped up the sludge which had spilt from a rancid pot of yogurt and a squashed, putrid banana. The bins smelt of festering fish and made the shoppers turn away.

It was the shoes she noticed first, the red sheen daintily avoiding the puddles as they scampered to find shelter. Rose faltered. Her heart stopped. The couple froze. Rose saw his electric flicker of recognition. His arm was held lightly around the woman's waist.

She dipped her tawny head towards him and pointed. "Isn't that the girl you mentioned? You know, the one who suddenly dropped out of your Art course?"

His brows furrowed, immediately to be swept away by a closed-in face as he shook his head and turned away. The woman who appeared to be his wife tapped him on the arm and persisted, "I'm sure it's her – all big canvases and grand ideas. Left suddenly as you said she couldn't cope with the demands of the course!"

Rose did not wait to hear the rest. She stabbed a squashed sandwich with her litter picker and crushed a coke can under foot.

The rain slid over her hood and ran in rivulets down her flushed cheeks. Despondently she trailed her debts and disappointments behind her, like the black bins.

Her gloved hand slipped as she tried to grasp a glass bottle, which spun in an arc through the air, before shattering into jagged fragments. She stopped. She stared at the prisms of light refracting off the sharp edges. In that moment she knew what she had to do.

Once Rose closed her bedsit door at three o'clock each day, she cocooned herself in her own creative world. In her hand she held a piece of charcoal and used sweeping upward strokes across sections of newspapers.

At night her head flew across the pages, swirling upwards, higher, further, straightening, before a flourishing finish; her world entwined in an intricate web.

She straightened her back, flicking her hair back behind her ears, examining the shapes from every angle.

Every day her mind planned, visualising the details; each evening she threw herself into the expression, firing her body into frenzied activity. Jewelled colours flowed through her hands, dripping in showers of sparkling rain.

Rose knew she was ready.

Her heart thudded as she stood outside St Benedict's College, dragging her bins behind her. She felt sick. Rose took a deep breath and pushed open the swing doors. At the back of the darkened hall she waited.

Some muttering arose from the students when her name was announced. She had deliberately registered her place on-line at the last moment, relieved that her Department of Education number was still valid.

She took a deep breath and stepped forward, dragging the grumbling bins, before carefully lifting a black plastic bag from each one and placing it on the stage. The background laughter and conversations seemed to blur in Rose's head as she climbed up the steps. She reminded herself that not only students and lecturers were seated in the darkness, but potential sponsors.

Rose moved forward on to the centre of the stage, enveloped now in silence and flanked by three large plastic bags. Someone from the back called out, "Look! She's brought all her rubbish with her!"

Rose let the sniggering subside, before fully emerging from the shadows. "Yes, that's right. I have." She had captured their attention now. "Everything I will show you this evening has been made almost entirely from recycled litter and natural materials that I have found."

She eased herself back into the darkness and slipped off the first black bag. Silence. Her heart hammered. She flicked the switch.

The lamp spun a golden pool of light into the gloom. Its shade was a bird poised for flight, the driftwood neck which was embedded with a glass mosaic, was outstretched. Its delicate shell beak was reaching upwards, the ruby glass eye gazing fixedly towards the charcoal sky. Behind it streamed a fan of feathers, each one made from intricately coloured paper clips, opening into plumes of saffron, russet and burgundy flames.

Rose let the Phoenix dance its way across the ceiling as the audience gasped, then she extinguished its fire.

Next she lit up an underwater world with blue green swirls dancing above and around the audience. Fish fins made out of plastic spoon heads, coloured with iridescent nail polish, flitted through wafting weeds, driftwood and shells; opalescent flashes in an inky gloom.

Rose paused before revealing her final lamp. There was a collective intake of breath. An oak stretched out its branches in an arc which encompassed the whole room. The tangle of twigs twirled into a tracery of spindly sticks, with glass green leaves glinting like sprites.

She flicked the switch off and stood still in the darkened room, holding her breath.

Only when she heard the roar of applause did she enclose herself in the centre to reignite the Phoenix, Underwater and Woodland Worlds, so that she was enshrined by the glowing lamps.

As Rose stepped off the platform she knew that whether she found a sponsor or not, she would find her own way towards a glittering, creative future.

Published in *Glit-er-ary*, December 2017, Bridge House.

Poppy, a Puppy for Remembrance

"Folk will know how large your soul is, by the way you treat a dog."

Charles F. Doran

She was not born on Remembrance Day, although I remember the day quite clearly. It was the day that Bill died.

His six closest friends and family traipsed into his cottage in a mournful procession, but by that stage he could hardly speak. It had seemed strange to me that we weren't greeted by his black Labrador, Megan. But then dogs have their own way of grieving. The two of them had been inseparable as she followed him like his sleek, silent shadow.

I leant over Bill's rasping body, wrapped in a crocheted bedspread. Shakily he gestured to his bedside table and I picked up a crumbling cardboard box. Gingerly I lifted the lid to reveal three war medals. He made some guttural sounds, mouthed repeatedly. I strained my ear towards him, but I could not decipher what it was that he was trying to say.

I moved back and gave an anxious look to Simon, his son, but he just gave a bewildered shrug.

It was his great grand-daughter who first heard them. A strange, high pitched yelping.

As Bill drew his last breath the sound became louder, more insistent.

We all stood still with our heads bowed in respect, too overwhelmed to register anything beyond that moment.

Outside a field of poppies stirred in the gentle June breeze. I imagined Bill's soul slipping through the corn field, brushing against the crimson petals and then taking flight.

32

I felt a small, insistent tug on my arm and I looked into the large olive eyes of Bill's great grand-daughter, Marie. "Come to the kitchen," she whispered.

We heard the little whimpers before even the door was open. There on the hearth lay Megan, surrounded by six sausage-like puppies wriggling and writhing.

So it was that we each received a puppy for remembrance, with Bill's son also keeping Megan. I decided to call my lively little black puppy, with her twitching inquisitive nose, Poppy.

Now a year on, I decide to walk through Bill's field once again. I park my car in a nearby lay-by, then we cautiously cross the busy road. Bill used to complain at the road kill, when reckless drivers regularly ran over birds, rabbits, even a deer.

Poppy is tumbling ahead of me, twirling through the corn. I call her back and she hurtles towards me, her tail thumping.

My fingers sink into her soft fur and I gently rub her chin. She nuzzles closer, her toffee eyes beseeching me for more.

Then off she bounds again; leaping like a deer over strands of corn, sniffing unusual smells and jumping backwards at the whirring of a pheasant's wings.

I think of Bill's rheumy grey eyes and soft smile. I used to listen for hours to his tales of endurance in battle, wrapped up as stories. Yet each time he heard an explosion: a car exhaust, a champagne cork or even the popping of some logs on his fire, he would flinch, turning into himself. His eyes would stare intently forward, his body rigid. Megan would lean her wise head on his lap and wait patiently. I would creep away, afraid to disturb his silent reverie.

Now he has given me a puppy to look after and who also cared for me. It was Poppy who helped me through when I dealt with the wrenching cramp-like pain of divorce. As I felt the door slam on my past, she would nuzzle her damp nose on to my lap and lift her soft padded paws over me. I found comfort in leaning my head against her gentle warm fur, knowing that she would never desert me.

Then there was the night of the burglary. Poppy had alerted me with her feverish barking, but they had still managed to steal all of Bill's medals.

I stood shivering in my nightie as the wind blew through the broken window. I clasped the empty battered box, turning it over in my hands. Poppy barked an angry tirade at the retreating figures and I felt Bill's loss once more.

Bill always used to say, "A dog's loyalty will never falter." I feel the watery June sun warming my arms. Poppy bounds around me in circles, keen to play. I try to hug her, but she wriggles free, keen to keep moving. She flits after a rabbit, then comes lolloping back, with her tongue hanging out.

We clamber up a hill, relishing the warmth and our freedom to roam. Poppy sniffs the air and I drink in the moment, me with my dog.

I run down the hill with my hair flying out behind me. Poppy jumps against my legs, barking excitedly, with her tail whirring.

We are breathless with happiness as we wind our way back through the edge of the poppy field. And then it happens. Without warning. They are hunting pigeons. The gunshot echoes around the valley. Poppy's eyes widen in horror.

Then she bolts. Futilely I call out. But she can only hear the throbbing fear in her head.

Blindly, recklessly she races across the field. Without a backward glance she slides through the hedgerow, hurtling straight towards the main road.

I scream her name. I bolt after her, stumbling clumsily in her wake.

The traffic noise booms louder, screeching nightmarishly and reverberating around the valley.

"Poppy!" I scream. Yet I know it is too late. "Poppy!"

I stand at the gate and stare.

In the middle of the bend I see another road kill. Another death that would not be noted. A strangled scream is stuck in my throat.

I creep towards the hunched over, matted fur. A scarlet rosette of blood encircles the body.

Another rabbit. So where is Poppy? I look across the road.

There she sits by my car. She looks up with liquid brown eyes that know she has done wrong.

I kneel down and wrap her in my arms. A dog's loyalty will never falter.

Published in *The Best of Café Lit 6*, August 2017, Chapeltown Books.

The Little Red Shoe

"Work like you don't need the money. Love like you've never been hurt. Dance like nobody's watching."

Satchel Paige

Drink to go with this story: Piicon Bière, created in 1830. This is a French orange bitter liqueur which also contains essences of gentian and quinin and it is mixed with pilsner or wheat beer or even Hoegaarden to make it particularly potent. (Quinine has been used for restless legs syndrome and gentian for hysteria.)

Impulses by their nature are difficult to explain but when Jocelyn enclosed the smooth wooden box in her palm and absently passed the money over, she didn't even attempt to. It was simply there, in a Strasbourg market, waiting for her to find.

Her ponderous footsteps meandered wearily between the stalls in Place de l'Etal, with the awning flapping to free itself above her head. Weighed down by the heat and her thoughts, her joints felt stiff and heavy, so unlike her younger years.

She scanned trestle tables of nougat and honeycomb, cheap oversized sunglasses and bubbles of beads that were suspended from wire racks. Some jewel coloured crystal goblets reflected the setting sun in taupe, amber and burgundy, burnishing her hair in the sheen of the golden light.

As Jocelyn sauntered away from the striped canopies, she heard a faint rattling sound clinking in time to her steps. Back in her hotel room she peeled open the lid, inhaling the musty oak smell. Nestled in a corner lay a small object, which she prised out with a finger and turned it over in the palm of her hand. It was surprisingly heavy with a silver hallmark at its base, a tiny pointed shoe, painted over in a vibrant red.

Without hesitation, she strung it on to the silver chain around her slender neck. Somehow it seemed appropriate, after all her years at the ballet. She had given so much to that life, not just her time, but her health and relationships. Single-minded ambition was essential when she had to shine above all the other dancers to be noticed and she could not slip for a moment or a new girl would be waiting in the wings to take her place. Such intense rivalry made it difficult to form firm friendships. Even when she pulled her tendons and strained her joints, she had to keep smiling. Even when John realised that he couldn't compete and the 'phone calls stopped coming. Wherever the venue, whichever the country, when the spotlight shone, she surged into life.

Her whole world had been poised on the point of a pirouette.

When it ended, she went on a tour of the places she liked best, but with heavier limbs and an aching hollowness inside.

That evening she wore scarlet to match her shoe and set off in search of a pavement café. Birds wheeled above her in the sky, dipping and diving in free, fluid movements. Her steps began to pat rhythmically as she walked and she found herself drumming her hands against her thighs in time.

At the Place Gutenberg, a carousel whirled around, spinning russet and gold horses with their hoofs lifted in an eternal gallop. Her head felt as though she was turning with them.

At the far end of the square, on a wooden raised platform, a jazz band was performing, not simply playing. Even at a distance, she noticed that their animation riveted groups of people strolling out for the evening, so that they stopped to watch and listen.

Jocelyn observed an elderly couple tapping their feet at a nearby pavement café. She found herself swaying to the music, her cotton skirt fluttering and swooping around her legs. Her body moved sinuously in its own dance to the natural rhythm. Her aches and inhibitions melted away, as all her senses became swallowed in the heat, the throbbing drum beat, the saxophone's insistent call, the trumpet's victory dance.

Soon she was surrounded by others who were also immersed in the moment. She forgot to eat or drink, aware only of her circling arms and swirling hips. Jocelyn noticed that the saxophonist seemed to be gazing in her direction, as though the sweet bursts of improvised harmonies were just for her. The tune surrendered to bottom base notes and her skirt billowed out around her like a balloon.

When the band stopped playing to drink beer, she continued swaying. The saxophonist attempted to flatten his unruly black hair, then assuming nonchalance; he tucked his hands into his pockets and strode over. His grin lacked the arrogance of so many of the men she had met in the past, but still she kept dancing to the background music played by the local café.

"I think I know you; I've seen you before, that is, I've seen you dance. Properly I mean." Realising his faux pas, he ruefully ran his hand through his hair so that it stood up in clumps, which made Jocelyn grin. "No that's not what I meant to say. You are Jocelyn Gatsby aren't you? The Prima Ballerina?"

Jocelyn smiled with a barely discernible nod.

"Your ballet dancing's stunning," he shook his head. "That sounds presumptuous, of course it would be, but this," he pointed to her dancing in the square, "I like it even better, it's freer, more flowing, less controlled. I'm Ted by the way."

She took his outstretched hand and led him into the dance. "Well Ted, the music's wonderful! How long have you been playing the saxophone?"

"Since I was eight. Drove my Mum mad at first. She wanted to know why I couldn't be normal and play the recorder like the other kids."

Jocelyn laughed. "Sometimes these interests can take over. It did for me until very recently. Do you travel much for your work?"

"It used to be all the time, but apart from this mini three week tour of Europe, I am largely based in London now. It was no life really, without any place to call home, or a person to call my own."

Jocelyn nodded vigorously, trying to stop the sadness from welling up inside.

His hazel eyes searched her face. "Is that why you stopped dancing on the stage?"

"No, a dancer's life is short lived. Like a butterfly, you have to make the most of your day in the sun. In the end I couldn't keep fighting against my injuries and younger feet stepped into my shoes."

"And now you're here and you can't stop dancing," he laughed, waving to a band member holding up his saxophone. "Have you been to the museum yet?"

"No, but I leave tomorrow lunch time."

"Well you should," he replied, stepping away. "Read about the St Vitus Dance," he called over his shoulder. "It happened exactly 501 years ago to this day, on the 15th June, 1518."

With a flourish of notes, he re-joined the band. She flitted amongst the twirling dancers as a soft velvety darkness slowly descended over the square, warm and comforting.

As the numbers increased, surging forward, her feet

sought greater freedom. A sense of panic constricted her, needing to escape Ted's gaze, no longer soothed by the saxophonist's melody. The cobbled road radiated outwards, splayed in a fan. She felt him watching her as her steps pattered rhythmically away and her hands weaved the air. Her skirt swept out behind, like a warning red flag.

She was spinning, whirling with her hair flailing out behind her in the flickering lights. Groups of students joined the dance, singing, shouting, ringing bells, blowing horns. At the Place Kleber they leapt into the fountains, leaping through the spray with gleaming droplets sparkling on their clothes.

They processed through Petite France, past Liquorice All Sorts coloured Tudor houses outlined with thick black beams. They shimmied beside the river Ill winding its silky sheen through the moonlight and underneath balconies laced with rich red geraniums.

As a torrent of water rushed through the loch gates, the group disbanded and Jocelyn stood alone watching the inky black River Ill. Almost in a trance, she found a bench where fronds of a weeping willow formed a fringe between her and the sweeping river. Shadows pooled around the path as the darkness thickened.

Jocelyn shuddered as her clothes clung clammily to her skin. Breaths of breeze rippled the willow, but she stared through its tentacles at the deep, dark River Ill snaking through the city. Flanked on both sides, the Tudor buildings slumped drunkenly together; she could almost hear their creaking timbers. Ripples of laughter trickled their way through from a distant back street.

Suddenly a cool hand touched her arm and she jumped up, stifling a shriek. His grip was firm, his eyes wide and dark. "Sorry, I didn't mean to startle you, I was just checking that you were okay, that's all."

40

"Okay? I was until you came along and frightened me out of my skin! Have you been following me?" She arched her back defensively.

"Following? No of course not. How could I? But I was concerned about you, when you went flying off like that. I wanted to check that you are all right. I'll go now if I'm not needed." He rose and Jocelyn could see that he was bristling.

"Sorry, no it's me. Please sit down. I don't know what has come over me this evening."

He looked concerned at her soggy clothes. "Look why don't I walk you back to your hotel before you catch a chill. It's easy to get lost in some of these dark back streets."

Jocelyn nodded and he planted a firm steadying arm around her back. She became aware that her skirt and top clung to her body. "Oh the wet clothes. We all ended up in the fountains at Place Gruber."

Ted grinned. "So what time's your train?"

"It leaves at 12.15," she sighed.

"Well that should just about give you enough time to check out the museum." Gently he kissed Jocelyn on the cheek and left her staring after his receding back.

The following morning her eyes flicked around the roads adjoining the museum for a man with unruly black hair. There was a ripple of laughter as a group of tourists flooded past, but he was not behind them. She couldn't shake off the pang of disappointment.

She tried to brush off the feeling of being stood up, as she pushed open the doors and slid inside. It was as though she had stepped back in time. Across the room, she noticed a picture of a pointed red shoe and swooped towards it. "St Vitus' Dance," read the caption. With a sharp intake of breath, she read the details of how a lone woman on the 15th June, 1518 set people in the town of Strasbourg compulsively

41

dancing. They did not stop for food, drink or even exhaustion. Various theories were suggested, from the rye bread, bacteria, collective hysteria to escaping the miseries of their lives, but to this day it remains a mystery. Eventually the dancers were led to the St Vitus shrine, where they were given red shoes and finally stopped their dancing.

With her heart thudding, Jocelyn fingered the red shoe around her neck. She knew what she must do. Carefully she slid it off her chain and ran to the market at Place de la Grande Boucherie, aware that her steps felt lighter, the aching had gone.

She elbowed past punnets of strawberries and plump nectarines. A stall-holder reclined in a chair in front of a trestle table laden with brass pots, his mouth open and his belly heaving. Jocelyn chose a tarnished vintage jar, embossed with a filigree of brass leaves. With a quick glance to the side, she lifted the lid, slipping the shoe inside it with a clink. Somehow she knew that the right person would find it.

Just as she was about to leave for the station a finely spun black silk scarf caught her eye. It rippled over her fingers as flimsy as gossamer. A cyan feathery design was etched across it, sprinkled with an iridescent gold shimmer, which danced in the morning light.

As Jocelyn opened her bag to pay, she noticed a card that someone must have dropped inside. It was for the Ruby Slipper Jazz Club and simply said, "I play here every Friday. Please come and dance. Ted x."

Jocelyn placed it carefully inside her purse and smiled as she sprinted for her train.

———————

Published on the *CaféLit* website, July 2019.

Rescue Me, Saving You

"Thorns may hurt you, men desert you, sunlight turn to fog;
but you're never friendless ever, if you have a dog."
Douglas Malloch

John Staines celebrated the first day of his retirement by buying his wife a shiny red Mazda. Then he stood back in his front garden as she drove off, out of his life in it, the metallic gleam disappearing into the sunset.

It didn't take long for John to learn that when Priscilla folded herself and her blonde bob into the driving seat, they hadn't gone far. She parked at Barney the plumber's at number 46; an acquaintance that had developed when their pipes had needed lagging.

All that was left of John's retirement bonus was the elaborate gilt and rather distasteful carriage clock that had been presented. It seemed he was given it to watch its interminable ticking, now that his life no longer needed to revolve around clocks. Time hung heavily.

The company retained Priscilla's services, but no longer had any need for his "pernickety perfectionism." Technology could deal with the more fastidious details. In any case, they could employ two younger people for his salary, a two for one deal.

John discovered that if he leaned out of his bathroom window, he could see number 46 quite clearly. He started to jog along the road and into the park, as though his speed would make the day move faster. Each time he would look in through their windows, memorising all the details.

One morning he slid along the park track with his head lowered, when he had a sensation of being followed. His hood was wrapped around his head and rain slid down his face. Mud slithered over his legs as his trainers slipped and squelched. There was a sniffing, snuffling, panting sound around his heels.

John looked down at a creature with mud mangled fur. He kept running. So did the dog, keeping perfect time. Never before had John been the recipient of so much attention.

At the end of the park the dog looked up expectantly. He was bedraggled, without a lead or collar, so John wound his scarf around the dog's neck and marched him to the vet's. No identichip was found and no reports of a missing border collie. It seemed as though they had found each other.

When the vet asked if she could record a name for the dog, he looked at its downcast tail, shrugged a sagging shoulder and said, "Droopy."

As John ran a bath for Droopy, he recalled how his wife hated any kind of a mess. He rummaged under the sink for his wife's favourite organic shampoo and rubbed a little into his fur. Droopy shook it out. Soon the entire bathroom, from the fitted ceiling lights to the white tiles was flicked with mud splats.

In the airing cupboard he pulled out the fluffiest Egyptian cotton towels to rub Droopy down.

Meal time was a little more problematic. Although he had bought some dog food from the vet's, he'd forgotten the bowls. Scouring the cupboards he found his wife's two favourite ceramic dishes which were an ideal size for a water bowl and Chunky Paws dog food.

John removed the lid off Priscilla's large sewing basket and laid it on the floor. He rolled up several of her softest cashmere jumpers – "cashmore" he used to call them as they had cost her a fortune. These could be the ballast at the bottom of the dog bed. He found a particularly downy alpaca scarf, which he laid over the top.

Droopy appreciated all of these preparations for his day

bed, but at night time he padded after John up the stairs and slept on his wife's side of bed.

Unable to sleep, John crept down the road. The metallic car winked provocatively in the street light. He waited until midnight when they switched off and then he attached some empty cans with string to the underside of the car. He wrote Just Married in Priscilla's favourite lipstick across the rear windscreen and as an extra, stuck the contents from one of the tins of sardines into the radiator grill. John knew that when she left the house at exactly 7.15 in the morning, that she would disturb all of the neighbours.

When he returned to snuggle up to Droopy, he slept surprisingly soundly, with just the dog's snoring reverberating around the room.

At first the two of them just mooched around together, until a neighbour's cat leapt into a tree next door. Droopy cleared the fence in seconds, and the next one and the rest of the row. Breathless, John caught up with him at the end of the road, but it gave him an idea.

He started to assemble an assortment of obstacles in his back garden, beginning with mini jumps. Droopy was fast and surprisingly agile. Next he added in a tunnel and coaxed him through it, followed by a hoop to jump through. Finally a row of bamboo canes made the weave, which Droopy learned to wind his body around at speed.

Every morning they eagerly practised, becoming faster and faster. But still he watched number 46 when he had time, assisted now by some binoculars he had bought.

On another sleepless night John crept into Barney's front garden, armed with a spray containing bleach and weed killer. For twenty minutes he sprayed the letters BASTARD across the lawn, adding a few extra flourishes. John had always been good at art at school and found the process immensely satisfying.

45

Droopy's training continued apace, particularly when they joined a couple of agility clubs. They learned how to use the A frame, dog walk and see-saw. As he fine-tuned their technique, he also taught Droopy to sit stay. The collie was quick and clever, the perfect pupil.

A few weeks passed in no time and they registered to take part in some trials, with a view to participating in competitions. John improved his own fitness, but also learned how to direct his own body language, as his dog responded to the slightest gesture.

Every day they improved their timing and sharpened their precision. So great was their absorption that they didn't hear a scribbled note being thrust through their letter box from Priscilla, requesting the return of her clothes.

John approached the task with his customary precision. He neatly folded the remaining items in Priscilla's wardrobe, carefully layering them with tissue paper. He added a few items of his own. These were placed in large boxes, all of which were labelled with her name in large bold lettering.

He unloaded the boxes into the office block around lunch time. Tony the doorman gave John a cursory nod, whilst Paula on reception smiled and buzzed Priscilla when he showed her the note.

He piled the boxes on top of each other, ensuring that P. Staines was clearly displayed. Just before he departed, he quickly reached inside and activated the sex toys hidden in the bottom boxes. He hastily slipped through the doors as the buzzing and vibrating began.

A moment later security was called, but John only threw a backward glance at the confusion. He was dimly aware of some sirens flashing in the distance.

Already John's mind was thinking about the qualifying Agility Competition, the one which could take them all the way to Crufts.

The pair moved like a single unit, with Droopy obeying every gesture, every command to twist, turn, jump. The angles were sharp, defined, precise. John's heart hammered at the speed, pushing them on further, faster, better.

He didn't see Priscilla amongst the spectators, bobbing around in her seat with excitement, not even when she gave a little wave or stood up to cheer amidst the roaring crowd when they won their round. It was just him and Droopy dog a.k.a. Mr Mud-Mangler-Give-Em-Welly.

_____

Published in *Crackers*, November 2018, Bridge House.

Alone at Avalon

"Be a loner. That gives you time to wonder, to search for the truth. Have holy curiosity. Make your life worth living."

Albert Einstein

"To escape from the world means that one's mind is not concerned with the opinions of the world."

Dogen

Sea spray was flung against the hull as the fishing vessel speared its way through the waves. The dull drone of the engine sounded to Konami like the hum of reporters, the glinting evening sun like the flash of their cameras and the seagulls' screams were their raucous accusations.

Had a fisherman recognised her as he looked up above his newspaper? Or was it just the anxiety hammering inside her chest? She lowered her hat still further and adjusted her sunglasses.

The waves thrashed and bickered below the boat, churned up by the motor to fling up stinging salty spray.

A grey mound loomed on the horizon, the tiny dot of an island. Three days. That was all she was taking, and two of those days included travelling time. A chance to get away from all the screeching demands. To mend.

Konami closed her eyes and tried to imagine absolute solitude. The sound and rhythm of the water was soothing. No emails, no phone, no television, no contact. No public image to worry about, or sly photos showing the cavernous hollows under her eyes. No more stories which held two threads of truth, enough to be convincing, and the rest fabrication. She could be alone, to just be herself.

Konami must have rested for she was jolted awake by

the knocking of the boat against a shoulder of rock. Strong arms reached down and pulled her ashore.

There it stood, alone against a landscape of rocks and trees, the grey stone of Avalon Cottage, offering little more than basic running water and electricity. Inside it was cool and quiet apart from the murmur of the sea. She pulled her bag onto the simple bed which was tucked under a thick-walled window and she watched the white spume as the craft pulled away.

She flexed her shoulders. Dusk was falling fast, spreading elongated shadows from the straggling trees. Silence. Peace. Konami broke off a piece of crusty bread left for her supper on an oak table, along with a chunk of cheese and an apple. She wondered when food had last tasted this good.

First, she would sleep, ready to explore the tiny island tomorrow. Konami watched the moonlight illuminate the room, dancing ripples upon the ceiling. Her limbs felt stiff, the bed solid and unyielding.

She knew that she was totally alone. That no-one could gain access to the island, except from the cove, which even now she could see from her bed, lit up by a path of moonlight. She knew that she would stir if someone depressed the iron catch on the front door. So why couldn't she sleep?

It was useless. She wrenched the loose white sheet off the bed and draped it around her body, almost stumbling over. It reminded her of the time when she had tried to make a dignified exit from the press who were clamouring around her for quotes. She rushed away from them but had tripped as her heel caught in her gown. How they loved those photos, with captions about her drinking!

Now she was entirely alone. Konami slipped on some glittery flip flops and followed the stream of silvery moonlight.

A gentle breeze rustled the bushes, swishing the leaves like fans. Deeper into the island she padded, parting ferns, aware of her vulnerability. A sudden screech froze her movement. A cat perhaps?

The trees smelt sweet, draped with overhanging blossoms in an orchard. In front of her lay the black sheen of a pool which seemed empty apart from the slithers of moonlight skimming off the surface. It drew her forward, the ripples winking, its depths dark and cool.

She leaned forward so that the tips of her hair almost skimmed the surface. A face glared back at her with wild, glinting eyes, sharp cheek bones and ragged curls. Konami yelped and leaned backwards, her heart thumping. That gaunt face with those intent black eyes was her reflection dragging her into the water. Her hair felt like anchors, trying to pull her under, heavier and heavier. The more she tried to reach backwards, the stronger the force forward, so it seemed that she only had to close her eyes, just once more.

Her body felt weighted with water, even though she was dry, as she hauled herself back to the cottage. She thought of the court case in three days' time. Then the agonising wait would be over, but the media attention would whirr up again. Journalists, like mosquitos would be humming around her, eager for a bite.

She stretched out on the bed as all sensations drained away and she sunk deeper and deeper into sleep.

Konami awoke with a jolt, cold and startled to see how long she had slept. The sheer silence, apart from the lapping waves, had swept her worries aside. Outside the window swirled a white sea mist, in which the house, sea and sky seemed to merge.

After a quick wash and some comforting porridge, she huddled herself into an oilskin coat that she found on a hook. With hesitant steps she followed the peninsula, but driven by the mist and the vertical cliff drops, moved inland. Even the sea seemed muffled and smothered.

The cold fog clung to her as she found herself again beneath the apple boughs, strewn with damp clumps of white blossom. As she knelt forward into the opaque mirror, tendrils of mist swirled around her face. It was lit in an ethereal glow. She stretched out her hands, white tentacles, as though belonging to another being, pulling at the miasmic wraiths, then clenched into empty fists.

Marble and motionless she froze in a trance, a blur of despair. The clammy, mucid vapour seemed to chill and transude her bones, leaving her empty and desolate.

Konami shook her head, stretched and rose, as though sleepwalking back to the house. A hot shower stung as it forced the blood to flow around her body and with it, warm tears. All of the blocked-up emotions flooded out, leaving her huddled on the floor, pink and raw.

Konami only had an hour before the skipper would return her to the mainland and she felt compelled to visit the lake once more. The mist had lifted to let an emerging sun filter through. In the orchard a sweet smell lifted in the air, as coral tinged white blossoms stretched in garlands and arches. The lake reflected back the sky's silvery sheen and her face, clear and strong. A sharp sword of light burst through the clouds as she reached her arms upwards; she felt infused, recharged and regenerated.

Nothing she could do would alter her past, but everything she did now would change her future.

A Sprinkling of Hope

"The key to happiness – as any good fairy godmother will tell you – is not to avoid problems, but to overcome them."

Janette Rallison

Sometimes in life, the right person comes into our lives at the right time. I am no Cinderella and I have not been living in a children's story, but it felt as though my Fairy Godmother had arrived at exactly the time that I needed her most.

Instead of waving a magic wand, Sheila gave a helping hand. Instead of arriving in a sprinkling of star dust and a horse drawn carriage, she swept up in a little blue mini with a ready smile.

It began with paid after school care, but soon became something infinitely more magical. We found ourselves whisked up into Sheila's special world.

On my return from work, I would smile to see my five year old daughter sitting on her haunches, turning over stones. Sheila would be sweeping her arms through the long grasses, whilst my son would be found dangling his legs half way up a tree. They explained that they were looking for fairies at the bottom of the garden.

Sheila's house backed on to an enchanted land with a bluebell wood, wild rabbits and games aplenty.

In the winter, Sheila's home became transformed into a Santa's grotto, in a whirl of Christmas lights, nativity scenes and snow dappled reindeer; not on December 25th, but at the end of January. All of the local children were invited to look around this sparkling wintry world, at a time when light was short and days were dark.

It was also a time when my days seemed dismal and difficult, but Sheila lit up my life too. Sometimes it was from a thoughtful comment, more often just from a look which resonated with understanding.

The children in turn, made Sheila glow, with their constant chatter, laughter, squabbles and smiles. Sheila confided to me that before we had soared into her life she had felt lonely. Now she had a purpose to get up in the morning, she felt valued and with a renewed sense of self-worth.

Sadly we lost Sheila to Parkinson's Disease when my children were still quite young. Her kindness and creativity live on in them now, as she showed them that there are no limits to imagination.

Sheila may not have sprinkled fairy dust, but she gave us hope that happier times would be ahead.

A tribute to Sheila Clay.

Published in *The Best of Café Lit 10*, August 2021, Chapeltown Books.

I Knew It in the Bath

"Some beautiful paths can't be discovered without getting lost."

Erol Ozan

The story takes place over just one hour as a woman reflects over the key moments in her life. The thoughts frequently revert back to the present moment as they link in with her actual bath time.

I have chosen the title of I Knew it in the Bath as it is the line that actors are reputed to say when they have forgotten their words. This parallels with real life, where expectations and intentions seldom match the reality. Sometimes we forget to use the script.

Above the steaming taps the spotlight bulb glazes the luminous body of Jessica Snow. Isolated by its beam, she is once again frozen in fear. Her throat constricts, the words are blown away like blossom. She shrugs helplessly, unable to play her part and declares, "I knew it in the bath!"

That cool encompassing womb that encloses all secrets, as safe as a confessional. Within the soothing balmy water her dreams can fly, her confidence can soar.

It's only when she will be forced to emerge, sleek and dripping from the comforting warmth, that she will feel exposed again. Quickly she will flick a towel over her nakedness. Then shivering she will fumble for the soft robe and wrap it tightly.

She feels the sensual anticipation with the clink of the bottle against the cool ceramic. A slight tilt and the creamy liquid splurges in; spluttering against the rush of tap water.

She swirls the water around, as she longs to cocoon herself in its frothy milkiness. Tentatively she dips her toes, then slowly, sleekly slides in, slipping silkily into a dreamy languor. This is her time, out of time, out of touch, untouched. Except for the thoughts pummelling inside her head, frothing over, then bursting like bubbles. A blink of the eye is like the shutter of a camera, a series of stills. Fragmented memories lie waiting to be pasted together like shattered porcelain. Or thrown, scattered, an urn full of life thrown to the wind.

She lifts a shrimp pink toe out of the water, breaking the line of perfectly formed bubbles. Once again she is dipping her feet into rock pools, sun warmed and mellow. Golden glimmering light ripples the surface, distorting her shell like nails. She throws her head back and smiles, the breeze catching her hair like a careless kite flung behind her. Nearby the thunderous sea spits out its furious spray. Seagulls scream and soar the sky in protest. But she is safe, twirling her toes in a rock pool.

Shouting voices and shrill cries are taken by the wind, lifted higher and higher; sparkling waves of life and laughter. Beach huts turn their paint palette faces towards the sea in a broad beaming grin.

With her arms outstretched she is soaring in waves of wind, wild and free. Her discoveries take her to the Moon's crust, where she poises on one leg in a crater, then dances into the eel like shadows of the sand.

She delights in watching her footprints disappear as she slinks across the gleaming gold. She makes a soggy imprint with one bare foot and watches the sand splurge and suck it down. She lifts her foot out and sees the soft cavity slowly rise and fill, like a sponge cake baking in her mother's oven.

A sturdy red plastic bucket is filled with smooth sand, and then tapped firmly down with a spade. Rubber dinghies bob resiliently upon the churning sea.

There is sand in her sandwiches. But still drunk with her dreams she sips on lemonade and gasps when the bubbles slip up her nose.

With slight fingers she cements her fragile sand castle together with pebbles, sticks and shells. Tottering paper flags flutter in the salty breeze. Purposefully she digs her protective moat, deeper and deeper. Instead of keeping out the invading force of the sea, it seeps in from below, dribbling between her toes and slipping into her clothes like blotting paper.

A sticky hand yanks her back to the shore, away from the slow sucking shingle and the sliding sorbet sun.

From the promenade she watches her fairy castle, melting like an ice-cream as it slips defenceless, oozing into the sea. The battlements sink in surrender on top of the soggy drowned flags. Greedily the sea runs its tongue over its ramparts, swiftly licking its mound into a memory.

Even the rock pools get swallowed and gorged, their shimmering golden glow submerged beneath the shuddering sea.

A flapping of cotton skirts bid good-bye, alongside a scampering of litter as she dismisses the tossing white spume.

Her fluttering eyelids also sweep good-bye to the childhood rock pools, although she can still hear the incessantly curling waves and the wheeling of the gulls.

Glittering sea spray, swirling water, waves of motion. She twirls the warm water around the bath tub.

The splash, her submersion, their first meeting. They spin, head over heels in a gush of water.

She flies, with arms raised along the water jet; in a rush of exhilaration. Bubbles, laughter and echoing cries resonate around the domed pool.

Screaming she is flung from the tube, cascading into the

water with a motion that is not her own. She is unable to catch herself as she is flung across his back. His eyes widen with surprise, as she collapses helpless with laughter.

She slips under water in a blur of voices and veiled vision. She emerges gasping for breath. A steadying arm reaches out and she looks into smiling blue eyes. Around them they hear the distant cries and screams, as shards of light crack the glistening, glassy water. But they are separate and safe, enclosed in their own bubble of time.

She sinks back in the bath with a sigh and raises a soapy hand to her forehead. A bracelet of bubbles slithers from her wrist.

She sees it all through a miasmic mist, as fragile as a web, as effervescent as a dream. She is a fairy tale princess, wrapped in a lacy haze of veils. Her hair is tucked inside a glittering tiara, away from her flushed pink cheeks. She looks as fragile and lovely as a wild rose.

She melts down the aisle in a mist of vanilla spray, which is frothing and foaming at her silk slippers. Her diamonds glint in shards of light. He encloses her hand and circles her finger. The gossamer gauze in her bodice flutters in flight at her breast, but she is ringed.

The moment is captured outside in an endless series of clicks. The heat is stifling. He holds a proud proprietorial arm through hers. In her other hand she tries to balance her heavily wilting bouquet. A cloud of confetti is blown away like blossom.

As she tilts more foam into the bath she remembers the clink of glasses once the champagne has been poured. It spills over the bowls in frothy bubbles of excitement.

She is soaring now, not on the wings of a gull, although they are circling overhead, but on a sleek white yacht. Their honeymoon. Its smooth curved sides slice through the waves, firing exhilarating spume against the deck. The spray shivers in anticipation before slipping back into the sea.

He stands proudly at the helm, controlling the boat's movements as it fights against the rhythm of the sea. He has plotted their course using the best navigational equipment, although they do not venture beyond the perimeter of the harbour.

He pats protectively at the seat which holds the life jackets, encouraging her to sit down. She fidgets, pacing around like a cat. Why can't she be still, even for a moment?

She smiles, acquiescing, but yearning to sit at the bow, with her arms tucked around her legs and her hair flying out like a spinnaker behind her.

At last they slip anchor and tie up next to a bobbing buoy. She pads up onto the roof deck and luxuriously stretches, lapping up the sun. Her eyes close as she is gently rocked by the dipping rhythm of the boat.

He sits up, shocked. She has tried to remove her swimsuit, for all the world to see, to condemn, her brazen nakedness. She shows no remorse, no modesty.

Laughingly she replaces her top, protesting that they are alone in their own watery universe; there is no-one nearby to disturb them. But her words are left helplessly flapping, like the lowered sails.

Below the deep green ocean churns its impenetrable gloom, dappled over with a flickering light.

She submerges into the cabin and he notes with pride its pleasing orderliness. He knows that in a yacht this size everything must be properly stowed away.

She emerges with relief upon the ladder, clinking some glasses together. The cabin smells stuffy and plasticky. In spite of the heat she wraps a robe around her body. It's only her face that she throws to the breeze and the fierce sun.

They had agreed that she would not return to acting. Her career, such as she had, was over. Not in the dimming of the amber lights, but through the interrogative laser beams of the press. He did not remind her of it of course, not directly. But she knew that she had reason to be grateful to him. As for the photographs, well they told their own story.

Yet those were her floaty days, when she seemed to glide through waves of rippling grass. She looked at the world through a shimmery, effervescent bubble. It shut reality out, reflecting it back in a myriad of glistening colours.

The golden glow of summer streaked the fields and glazed her dark hair with a honey haze. Dizzy with laughter and wine, they stumbled together in a pool of purple clover.

It wasn't that she had not been warned about him; they said that he was dangerous. That was part of his attraction.

She had been shivering on the hillside as the blustery wind flapped her skirt. The filming had taken ages. She was always waiting, waiting, though she had so little time.

The producer sat on the side-lines watching it all, supposedly in the background, but observed by everyone. His black hair was swept back behind him and he had a wry smile on his face. He had the aura of the man who linked all the chains, made the important decisions.

Then soundlessly he had stolen up behind her and firmly encircled a rug around her shoulders. She gave a start and then smiled up at him. It could have been a mink. Later they used that rug again.

It's strange how his presence seemed to invigorate her, whilst others sapped her soul. For people, she often thought were like planets or black holes. Some people had a gravitational pull as they reflected light and energy. Others were more deceptive, hidden black holes that sucked in and destroyed.

But he was bursting with a big, bold light, more like the sun. He exuded a powerful pull of electromagnetic energy and all the other planets revolved around him.

There were some of course who got scorched by him, or who withered in his over powering heat. But now she was standing on the hillside, basking in his light.

The work came pouring in. For she glowed in his warmth and his attention, at last she was noticed, shining in his beam. It seemed as though nothing could touch her as she spun in the pleasure of her own motion, radiating golden sparks like a Catherine Wheel.

Then rumours rippled like a breeze across a cornfield. A dark brooding storm crossed his brow and his eyes clouded.

Faces turned away from her, eye contact was no longer held. Contracts started to fall through, her agent became too busy to return her calls.

No longer did she stand in a golden pool of his light. Encroaching shadows crept across and covered her. She shivered in fear as her confidence evaporated.

They condemned her, as only those who truly believe in their own goodness can. The papers carried pictures of his wife and children, gazing out with liquid, admonishing eyes. Slashed to the side she brazenly stood, luridly clad in scarlet. In time she knew that she would read of another who had floundered in his hidden shallows.

Her associates bent together, stooped like poplar trees, with the whispering of their leaves thrown to the breeze.

The greater their secrets, the more they trampled on hers; the more intense their personal misery, the greater their interest in hers.

So she stood like a slender stem in the field, a frothy dandelion clock which had been blown by the wind; slipping away into invisibility.

Hands that have been in hot water too long burn and then they shrivel.

Somehow the moment never seemed right, but she had to tell him, she thought as she plunged her red raw hands back into the washing up bowl. She would choose her time carefully, after dinner perhaps, but before he picked up the evening papers. As long as his mother didn't phone; she so often did on a Friday evening. Just as they were getting comfortable, settling back to watch a film and then they'd hear the imperious ring. He would groan, but leap with alacrity from the sofa. And that would be the end of their evening together.

She ground the rough scourer around a saucepan. Or he would go scurrying back to the office. There were so many papers to shuffle. How would she know? How could she possibly understand? Stuck at home, with only domestic duties. She should consider herself lucky. Only someone thoroughly spoilt would complain about leading a life of leisure.

Often he'd heave himself out of his chair complaining of a bad back or his sinuses would be troubling him again. And really if she'd anticipated his needs properly she'd have bought in extra honey and menthol. She could be very inconsiderate.

She bit her lower lip. Sometimes she found it helped if she clenched her fists and dug her nails into her hands.

Of course some evenings he just wanted to get away from her. He needed his leisure, he'd earned it. And as his mother was so fond of telling her, "John does love his sport." Really it's only reasonable to let him have some fun, when he has to work so hard during the day.

How would he greet her news anyway? She'd been careless and really she had no excuse. She stroked her growing roundness, thrilled and frightened by the new life growing inside her.

She rung out her sponge, but it was the dish cloth that she saw in her hands. And even if he did turn away from her for a bit, because after all it hadn't been his decision, he'd get used to the idea eventually. Once he had time to make his plans, then it would be all right. Roughly she dried her hands and shrugged a cardigan around her shoulders.

She pours in a jet of steamy water which whirlpools at her feet. Using her hands as paddles she whirls it around, turning rivulets into ripples, ripples into waves; sucking and surrounding her body in a circling nest.

"Breathe deeply," he urges. "Don't forget to breathe."

Stupid advice, for she seems to have no breath, not even to curse. A birthing pool, the right thing to do; so natural, so serene.

The tightening band of pain is merging with the baby's heart. Wave upon wave; deeper and darker in intensity. The pulsing life is eager to escape its rhythmic, warm protective sac. Gradually the grip tightens, bursting into an excruciating crescendo. She gasps and pushes, at first riding the wave, then submerging into it, drowning in a sea of agony. She yells, "Sod the birthing pool; get me an epidural!"

Gasping, sinking. A wave of life comes crashing to the shore. A reverberating scream echoes around the room. Then she holds her pink, helpless baby, his fragile soft skin cushioned against her body.

Her eyes melt at his tiny, tightly clenched fists. A searching little mouth is clinging like a clam, keen to feed. She is swept by a wave of overwhelming love. Their hearts beat in the rhythm of the moment. Keen to keep him safe, she circles him in her protective arms.

She swirls the bath water into rivulets that flow freely through her fingers; scuttling like crabs.

So she returns, like the relentless ocean pounding the

shore. Their arms are outstretched, taut with carrying blankets, brollies, laden bags and waterproofs.

Her exposed eyes squint at the watery sun as it slips behind the hazy clouds. Purposefully they stride across the endlessly stretching sands which are miraging into the sea.

He points. They stop. They deposit themselves in the spot, marking their territory.

He checks the sand, the wind direction, the tidal times. You can't be too careful. Out pour the nappy bags, the gritty sun lotion, insect repellent and sun glasses. Safe from the elements they huddle together, enclosed by their wind shield.

Already the bath water has cooled. She leans back against a boulder of frothy bubbles and sighs.

So her mother-in-law makes her weekly visit, punctually at 9.00. There is no need to answer the door, for she has her own key.

Hurriedly she wipes the egg yolk from Tommy's mouth and clears up some splattered food from the floor.

The mother-in-law makes her inspection, taking it all in, the pile of dishes at the sink, papers sprawled across the sofa and toys spilt all over the floor. She blows a floating kiss to Tommy, who will get a hug when he is properly presentable.

But Tommy won't be cleaned and he won't sit quietly. He is fractious as he always is in the presence of the mother-in-law. His face pinks and puckers as the tantrum prepares to erupt. Egg is flung across the floor, the sofa, the lamp shade.

She heaves him out of his highchair and tries to engross his attention in a children's story. For a moment they are together, their heads bent in caring communion. It is a Fairy Story and Tommy likes the pictures. In his excitement he flings the pages open, wildly, at random. And really he should begin backwards, with the girl marrying a handsome prince, only to discover that she's just kissed a frog, then yearning to wake up, to discover that it's just a dream.

Her mother-in-law shuffles impatiently on the sofa, for she can only endure so much indolence. "I don't like to interfere dear, and I'm sure you've got your own way of doing things." This said with a snort, the way a bull widens its nostrils when it is preparing to charge. "But I really do think that you should try to be more organised."

She has left the room, but the odour of her presence remains.

Perched at the side of her bath is a yellow plastic duck with a squashed beak. It can't float very well anymore, not since Tommy bit into its backside.

Later on Tommy rejected it, announcing that ducks are brown, boring sludge brown, not bright yellow.

When is it that we lose our capacity for colour and shape? When does our life become dull and blurred at the edges?

To a child a train is an exciting assortment of shapes in primary colours: red rectangular carriages, round green wheels and a yellow cylindrical funnel. To an adult a train is just a grey blur.

Tommy the commuter now restlessly paces the platform, glancing at his watch to check the time. A drizzly mist falls, blurring the edges and blunting all feelings.

Tommy will weave through the underground, oblivious of the haze of faces. He will scramble through the rush of people, deftly dodging shapes, scurrying into the gap. Like Sisyphus he will perpetually trudge up and down the escalators, heaving his weary form, carrying the shackles of his life, never reaching the top.

In his office pay roll his employees are numbered, their output is carefully calculated. And he will work and work, unrelentingly, until the day comes when he too will lose his productivity.

Uneasily she shifts in the bath, banking up against a wall of bubbles.

She's bending over a box, her face in a veil of tissue. They are moving up in the world, to a bigger house. He has made all of the arrangements, but now she must show less of the slack dreaminess, more purposeful activity. She can't expect him to do all of the work. But really the heat is so suffocating.

Row after row of boxes stand sentry in the hall. Reproachfully the labels lie ready to be stuck in place.

Wearily she lifts a sheet of bubble wrap and winds it around her wrist. She knows that she disappoints the perfectionist in him sometimes.

He covers the hall in a few quick, purposeful strides, glaring at her languor. She opens the flap of a box, staring into the gaping mouth which is waiting to be fed.

He scoffs at her childishness, at all the rubbish that she has gathered over the years; silly trifles, unnecessary tat. Lightly they are covered in a gossamer mist of tissue paper, and then packed side by side. The box is firmly shut; there is a wrenching of brown tape, at last it is sealed, safe from the elements.

His head flicks back and forth at the pretty woman on the television; he smiles adoring her witty comments.

She tears off more wrap to enclose a family photograph. There they stood, neatly in a row, poised plasticine people, smiling on command. A click and the moment is kept; Tommy's childhood is encapsulated in a respectable rectangular frame.

She remembers that day clearly; somehow she just couldn't get things together. She was drudge weary from too many sleepless nights. Lunch had been cooked in an abstracted lethargy; the carrots had bubbled over, frothing across the cooker and burning the hob. He sighed.

Then she managed to spill some sauce on to her top and he clicked his tongue impatiently, for now it meant that she would have to change her clothes yet again. Various items were already sprawled across the bed, drooping like limp rags, until finally she had decided on a plain black jumper.

He frowned as she walked down the stairs. He did not criticise her.

She remembers when she too stood in the limelight, not packed away.

Absently she begins bursting the bubble wrap, enjoying the satisfying pop as each globe flattens. He scowls at her drooping shoulders, sagging jowls and grey elasticated waistband.

She holds it inside, breaking a fistful of bubble wrap which bursts the constrained silence in a bitter explosion.

So too, in the bath she kicks against the bubbles, but as one breaks another is formed.

She has escaped. She knows it's wrong. But it's really only a coffee. It is such a long time since they last met and it's not as though they would be alone together. It was quite a coincidence, bumping into him at the station like that. Why shouldn't they want to catch up, to hear each other's news after all this time? And he has been very successful; she had seen his name on plenty of credits. Of course she is going to be a little bit curious. And really, what could be more innocent than a quiet cup of coffee in a café? The guilt seems such a small price to pay for the thrill, the electrical charge which flows right through to her fingertips.

Then there's his intense, unfaltering gaze, flattering and attentive. He will notice the way that she has combed back her hair and the curve of her new red dress. And it's not just him. For suddenly she feels vibrant and attractive again, like a new life is pulsing through her. She tingles with the exhilaration of shedding her old skin.

Hurriedly her heels clatter along the street, following her steaming breath. Her hair is flung out behind her. She turns the collar of her coat up against the cold and she buries her pink nose inside.

At last she scuttles towards the door, gasping in the warmth as she melts inside. Her only greeting is from the boiling urn and the shiny table tops, but still she smiles, her cheeks flushed with a rosy glow of anticipation.

Wedged behind the counter is a round faced assistant, his expression as bland as a coaster. She muffles her order, almost guiltily, before shuffling to a corner and gazing out of the steamy window.

On each table, in a single glass vase stands a pert red carnation. How she hates carnations, with their fake, pointy, papery petals. Her pink fingers wrap like tentacles around the creamy cappuccino. She curls her slender neck towards the frothy, creamy bubbles, as they burst one by one.

He is habitually late as he hates to be kept waiting. And wait she would. Outside the streaming flow of traffic keeps up its heaving flow of movement. Outside the world is chugging and turning. Inside her stomach is churning. But she cannot move. Not until all her bubbles have burst, and perhaps not even then.

As she leans back in her bath she shuts her eyes, shrouding herself in darkness. Luxuriously she stretches out her limbs. The windows are steaming, stark white against the velvety black sky.

Night cloaks their special secret, wrapping it softly around them like sweet summer dew.

Stealthily she steals through the streets of shifting shadows and torrid dreams. Her heart thumps with suppressed ecstasy. She is drawn like the tide, pulled towards his beckoning finger.

She shudders as the screeching of an animal reverberates, shattering the silence. She sighs. Waiting, wishing, it flames.

She remembers that moment, just knowing. Swiftly a glance is exchanged between blazing, coal black eyes. Sweet silence, it promises such treasures.

They fly together like ravens, deep and dark. Lips are parted in a smile, a guilty grimace, in silence. They cling together, then let go.

Through the streets as dark as an empty stage set they creep; matching echoing footsteps, blanketed by the balmy night.

Inside his gleaming car their shuddering breaths steam the windows. They burn in the agony and the ecstasy of wanting. Two flickering embers merge into one flame. She's unable to stop, but she knows that it cannot continue. Frantic fingers are fumbling, soothing and stroking. A shadow flickers across the window panes, a sultry silhouette of their dreams and desires. The inky shapes are fluidly forming and spinning in their own motion.

Expelled into the now chill night air, she watches her steaming breath evaporate. The frosty silence is shouting. She knows that there is no beginning, only an ending.

The front door shudders shut. A dark, surly umbrella stares at her with pointing fingers. She hears black recriminations in the reproachful silence. So she buries herself into the deadly, deep impenetrable darkness, screaming inside.

In a glistening sweat she dreams; tossing and turning, feverishly murmuring. She reaches for a shadow that cannot be caught, whimpering as it slides between her fingers. The ebony hair merges with the night, long and glistening and gone.

She lies back, allowing her hair to trail in the bath water like weeds. Ophelia like, she dips under then rises; a crown of bubbles forming around her head. Like a wave, the water breaks over her, engulfing her body. She feels as though she is slipping under a silk coverlet, sliding, melting.

She tries hard to focus her dark eyes on the number disc on his jacket, trying to make sense of the sequence, to find some sort of order to things.

He perches awkwardly and oversized on the edge of her sofa. There is a lady too; she is vaguely aware, making cups of tea in her kitchen. Both present bland, careful faces.

She realises that the police officer is speaking, but his voice seems to come from far away. She recognises the appeal in his tone, the need to find an explanation.

"He had all of the correct safety equipment. His harness was secure; all of his navigational aids were working properly. It was just one of those strange things, a freak accident."

He studies her rock-like immobility. Lowering his voice slightly he leans forward. "There is just one thing that we don't quite understand." His face is calm, showing studied patience. "Why did he venture out then?"

Why then? He would have followed all of the shipping reports. Why would such a careful, meticulous man decide to sail in force 9 gales when storm warnings were on the national news?

She stares back at their hands clasped in thoughtful, professional concern. Then she closes her eye-lids to present a blank screen. They must not see the flickering images inside her head.

He snaps his book shut. There is a finality, a closing chapter. He will log the paper work, the name, time, date and incident number.

In a wave she sees his doughy face, coated with fine white foam. His bloated, pallid skin is as waxy and lifeless as an extinguished candle.

His ashes are thrown to the swollen grey sea. It crashes into gaping black caverns, spitting venomous spray. Like confetti he is taken up by the blustery wind, hurled up into the ashen sky.

Still the sea continues its heaving pulse of death, its endless pull at the churning shingle.

What chapters of his life would his glazed fish eyes have seen as he stared downwards into the jade water? Which lightning images would have been lasered across his mind?

With a flick of her foot she tugs at the plug chain. The water is churned into a groaning black whirlpool. A pale segment of warn away soap is caught in the torrent and plunders into the depth, submerged, drawn under.

Her feet leave damp imprints upon the white tiles, slowly to be sucked into the wraiths of steam, leaving nothing behind.

She shivers, she cannot get warm. Even shrouded in the soft creamy towel her body is as cold as a statue. The last glistening drops of water slip off her alabaster skin and fall.

Published as second place winner in *Something Hidden*, November 2013, Bridge House.

Hurricane Rosie

"Dogs do speak, but only to those who know how to listen."

Orhan Pamuk

There was a thud and a flurry of fur. A book was flung from side to side, its flailing pages feeling the full force of hurricane Rosie.

Mangled tissues were thrown in the air, flew up and fell like spume.

The eye of the storm sought new targets, a chewed table leg, a scratched rug and a mud splattered sofa.

The rudder tail wagged her with delight, as she steered towards me and stole my shoes.

I circled my arms around her body which was as soft as thistledown. With a shuddering sigh she snuggled on to my lap and closed her eyes.

Rosie, my perfect puppy.

—————————

Published in the *CaféLit Magazine* on the 3rd January 2018.

Shadow Play

"Knowledge is power, if you know it about the right person."

Ethel Watts Mumford

I pressed myself into the dark alcove, allowing the cold, dank wall to seep into my skin. As my breathing settled, so did the rhythm of the great house; the final few doors snapped shut, timbers creaked and the darkness thickened.

I waited until his lordship had caressed his whiskey glass a little longer, while he sat in front of his study fire. A good servant knows how to choose the right moment.

Poor Meg simply wasn't skilful enough. I watched her emerge from under the trees in her dew soaked gown, as a horse and rider cantered towards the stables. I could not see Lady Radford's face but her horse seemed startled, although she managed to pull on the reins to steady it. I had also observed her ladyship riding to Lord Melbourne's manor house some nights. She had recently dismissed her maid Alice in a fit of rage, after she had flung her satin slippers at her. Meg was quick to grasp the opportunity to manipulate her knowledge of her ladyship's nocturnal activities to gain a place in her service. I had tried to warn Meg that the lady would never truly countenance her in such a superior position.

Lady Radford's screech runs through me still, as the call ran out through the estate that some of her most valuable jewels had been stolen. Meg scuttled away, understanding full well what this meant for her. She did not escape far on foot. It was of no consequence that she was innocent, or that the jewels were not found on her person; she was caught in the act of guiltily slinking from the grounds. Meg whimpered as rough arms hauled her away. In shame, her head hung down from a limp neck, like a broken snowdrop, but at least a noose was not placed around it.

Lady Radford played the part of benevolent nobility and arranged Meg's release, but sent her on her way without even a character reference, banishing any hope of her obtaining another position. The household searched the manor and grounds for days in an attempt to recover the missing jewels. I didn't, I watched. I assumed that Lady Radford intended to find them herself at a later date.

With silent footsteps, I placed myself where I was most needed and it was my calm composure that persuaded Lady Radford to use me temporarily as her maid, until a more suitable replacement could be found. My hands looked rough from hard labour, but I knew how to dress her hair prettily, darn neatly and to set out her fine silks to advantage, all done as silent and insignificant as a shadow.

Knowledge is power, but it's also dangerous; it has to be led like a wild bear restrained in chains.

My garret room is cold, with little respite from the blasts of the northerly wind, but it affords me a view for miles, across the estate and beyond. Most nights the countryside is enclosed in a deep, dense darkness, but her ladyship would wait for the illumination of the full moon.

Early the next day, the chambermaid stoked the embers of the fire in her ladyship's chamber, while I laid out her scarlet gown. In repose she looked so peaceful, with soft curls against a rounded cheek, almost cherubic. I went downstairs to collect my wages, for my replacement was due to arrive the next morning. No-one in the household would even notice my absence.

As I peeled myself off the wall, I could feel the weight of my plan pressing into me, constricting my breathing. Yet I knew that I could ill afford to let this chance slip away.

I gave a tentative knock on the oak door and slowly turned the brass handle. The intense heat was stifling. I knew that it was unseemly to see his lordship at this hour; there could be dire consequences, and so my trembling was genuine.

"Begging your Lordship's pardon, but I have had such a fright! Whilst taking the air this evening, I was asked to deliver a message."

His shaggy eyebrows shot up.

"I was so frightened it took my breath away; I have not uttered a syllable of it to another person. A gentleman blocked my path and said, 'You will deliver this message to Lord Radford.' Before I could utter a startled cry for help, he covered my mouth with his hand and said, 'Tell him to watch for his wife at the break of dawn, on the night of the full moon, for he will see her riding out from Lord Melbourne's manor.' I could scarcely scream before he was gone and now I am quaking, not knowing what this is about." The pitch of my voice rose.

His complexion was ruddy, already heightened by the log fire and his whiskey. He stood up, looming above me. "What manner of man was this to stealthily creep into my grounds? A footpad?"

I knew that I had to dampen the embers of the conversation and leave it to smoulder a little longer, so I whispered, "That's the strangeness of this m'lord. His looks and demeanour were closer to that of a gentleman, more footman than footpad."

He stretched his neck over me, like a viper preparing to strike. "No gentleman would deliver secretive messages!"

"Begging your pardon sir, but the matter was delicate. Perhaps he was afraid of evoking your wrath?"

He bridled and reached to pour himself another whiskey. I feared that the crystal decanter would shatter in his tightened grip. As the liquid scorched his throat, I added, "My mind's in such a quandary, I know not what to think! If I may be so bold your Lordship, it might be better to rest a while and see what the dawn brings…"

His eyes burned into mine as he raised his arms. "You may leave!" I rushed out through the door and took a deep breath.

There was little time left and first I had to examine m'lady's chamber. I risked lighting a candle with a flint. The empty bed received only a cursory glance and I was grateful that I had already checked the most likely hiding places. Only one remained; the scrivener table, which was too heavy to contain only letters and papers. I prised the drawers open with a clip and placed stones inside to retain the weight. I pulled out a hessian sack from beneath my gown and poured the gleaming jewels inside, watching the sparks of colours as they clinked against each other; no time to admire them now. I tied the sack below my bodice, under my skirts, my heart thudding with every passing moment. Long shadows threw themselves against the walls.

Just as I was about to move, I heard echoing footsteps. I extinguished the candle and froze. A thunderous knock shook the door. If I were caught in here at this hour, my fate would be worse than Meg's. I scarcely breathed, grateful only that I had the foresight to turn the key inside.

Only when I heard the thumping feet recede down the hallway did I quietly turn the lock and peer out.

There was no time to waste as I rushed towards the stables, for I had to arrive before the ostler attended to the horses.

I pulled my thick worsted cloak around me as there was a sharpness in the air. The horses were already whinnying as I looked for the bay mare. I should have been more alert, more careful. I did not notice the dark shape move from the side of the stables. I was seized from behind and lifted into the air. I strangled my scream as I stared into the fury of Lord Radford's bristling face.

He shook me like a rag doll. "You have come to warn her ladyship! Do you deny it?"

"I beg your Lordship's forgiveness; I was only seeking to protect her, for she will be leaving Lord Melbourne's manor now." I flung an arm in the direction of the path she would take. He swept me aside as he leapt onto his snorting stallion and followed the brow of the hill.

My whole body was trembling in the chill morning air. I counted six beats before leading out the mare and mounting her. With a hurried glance behind I leaned into the horse's flanks and cantered towards the copse. She kicked up a cloud of earth in our wake. I hoped to be early enough to clamber onto one of the carts leaving for the market towns.

I would not be followed though, as I had created enough of a diversion. Lady Radford will be angered at the theft of her jewels, but what will she be able to do? Her reputation has been sullied and she could hardly declare that the same jewels had been stolen twice.

I had committed theft, but she had stolen Meg's life. The knowledge gleaned from my observations gave me the power to change mine.

Winner of the Historical category in the Globe Soup 7 Day Writing Challenge, around the theme: Knowledge is Power.

All that Glisters...

"All that glisters is not gold—
Often have you heard that told.
Many a man his life hath sold
But my outside to behold.
Gilded tombs do worms enfold.
Had you been as wise as bold,
Young in limbs, in judgment old,
Your answer had not been inscrolled
Fare you well. Your suit is cold."

William Shakespeare
Merchant of Venice, Act II Scene 7

The baubles, iridescent and fragile shimmered in the light. Thin as egg shells, they were illuminated by myriads of sparkling colours; yet they were robustly round, so that a careless flick might send them bouncing on the floor.

How different the tree looked now.

Sophie recalled the bare branches of the glossy fir, stark green against her freshly painted walls. She was determined to celebrate Christmas, even if she could only afford to buy the tree and would have to gradually scrimp and save to buy the decorations. At least it had roots, so that she could put it out in the garden afterwards, to use again next year. Perhaps by then, she would feel as though she too had laid some roots.

She inhaled deeply the sweet pine scent and it sent her spinning back to Christmases of her childhood; brightly lit, noisy, alive, not listening to the ticking of a clock. Working from home was useful, but quiet.

At times she felt as though she was plunging through a hollow tunnel of darkness. In an unknown town, she was the stranger; there was no familiar face, friendly nod or warm embrace.

As Sophie slipped along an anonymous supermarket aisle she felt like a shadow of herself, without substance. Her mind went blank. She couldn't think what to buy. Canned, bland tunes blew like a bubble about her.

She would start with an elderly neighbour's list, that was easiest. As she crossed off each item, she picked up whimsical fare for herself: chestnuts – she hadn't eaten those for years, tinned apricots, cranberry cheese. It occurred to her that she now had the freedom to eat whatever, whenever, she liked. This propelled her movements, so that they became swifter, more decisive.

There was a contentment to be found in little things: the smell of fresh coffee, sunlight streaming through the window and most of all snuggling up to Barney, her recue dog.

Little by little the pain of the past calmed to a dull ache; hours could pass without thinking of Mark's betrayal.

She kept busy by helping out in her community and it gave her a strange satisfaction, taking her mind away from her own troubles. When driving into town, it was simple enough to give lifts to a couple of people in her close who would normally walk or catch the bus. When she saw that the young couple next door were looking harassed, she cheerfully offered to look after their little girl, Angela, for a few hours, which they messily spent with paint, paper and glue.

Walking Barney, it was easy enough to take a couple of extra dogs belonging to her elderly neighbours. Barney brought with him a whirl of chaos and confusion: chewed furniture, scuffed carpets, pointed little teeth and a soft bundle of love. He would race towards her across the fields with his ginger ears flapping against his fluffy, cloud-like body and she would surprise herself by smiling.

All the while she knew that she must build up her inner

strength to barricade Mark out. Far too many times she had heard his false promises, the earnest pleas and she had believed him, because she wanted to. And he had known it. Just as he had always known how to prey upon her weaknesses.

Then a strange thing happened. Little gifts started to appear on her doorstep when she went out, wrapped in an assortment of tissue paper. The first one was covered in old crackly yellow paper and so Sophie was not expecting to find much inside. Instead she gasped as she unfurled its cylindrical shape. The glass was as thin and wispy as a cobweb, skimming over a shell pink dotted sphere. Carefully she placed it upon her tree where it winked its secret in the light.

The next day she found another parcel. This one had jewel coloured glass in ruby, emerald, sapphire and amber, etched around in encrusted glittering silver. It spun upon the tree branch refracting multi-coloured globes across the ceiling.

With a flutter of excitement Sophie discovered another one the following day, after her dog walk. She looked around, but no-one was in sight. *Could she have a secret admirer?* Her fingers fumbled to prise open the tissue paper. Inside was an oyster pink and cream porcelain bauble, with ribbed sparkling sides. As she gazed into its gleaming depths she thought, *surely this must be old? The tracery is so very fine, with thin vein like seams; I've never seen anything like it.*

Sophie found herself looking out for these tissue papered wrappings appearing on her doorstep, like flurries of snow.

It was only on Christmas Eve that she finally understood. A large mass of paper festooned in tinsel, was spun around a tennis ball shape. Inside Sophie saw a papier mâché bauble daubed in pink and purple paint, liberally splattered with glitter. Inside Angela had left a sugar paper card with a Christmas tree on the front. She had written: "Dear Sophie, thanks for helping us and all the neighbours. Here's a little gift to brighten up your tree. Love, Angela xxxx."

Sophie smiled as she selected a sturdy branch to hang it upon, then sat back on her haunches to admire the tree. The effect was unusual, as each glistening globe vied for attention, yet the burnished glow was warm and made her feel part of the community. She had prepared herself to spend Christmas Day alone, but this made her feel stronger.

She had not realised that this would soon be tested.

When a courier knocked on her door and delivered a wooden box, she was not at first on her guard. It was heavy, so she put it on the floor and lifted the lid of the straw lined box. Snuggled inside were individually hand-made baubles, encrusted with crystals in snowflake designs. She lifted each one out in turn, spinning them in the light as the leaf gold filigree flickered.

Firmly she replaced the lid and braced herself for the knock on the door that would surely follow, once he was sure that his gift had worked its magic.

She saw the sleek silver Jaguar slide into the parking bay before he appeared. Hastily she ran her hands through her hair and smudged on some lipstick. Sophie knew that she shouldn't care, that his opinion should not matter to her. She ran upstairs to change out of her jeans.

Her heart started hammering and before she knew it, he was standing on her doorstep, a wry smile on his face, hands in his pockets. Mark tilted his head to one side. "I hope you liked your early Christmas present. Aren't you going to invite me in?" An arched eyebrow showed that he knew the effect he had on her.

As though nothing had happened, as though she had not been torn into pieces.

Sophie edged to one side of the door and closed it with a click, as Barney bounded forward. In a flurry of fur and panting excitement he bounced against Mark's legs. Sophie noted with some satisfaction that his paws were still muddy from their walk and were being plastered against Mark's designer jeans.

With a satisfied sigh Mark sprawled on her sofa, dusting down his long legs. He gave her tree a critical glance. "Looks like my box of baubles arrived just in time. Now you can get rid of those tatty bits and put something more classy on your Christmas tree." He clinked two of the old baubles together as they clashed. Rocking rhythmically they swayed to and fro, the refracted light shimmering like broken glass on the ceiling.

Sophie felt a surge of anger, and with it, strength rise in her as she stood up and strode to the front door. He followed, confused, as she passed the wooden box back to him. "The baubles that you see on the tree have all stood the test of time. Unlike you."

Mark's blue eyes stared, as cold as marbles and his thin mouth curved into the subtlest hint of a sneer. "You've changed," he said.

"Yes and I'm going to continue changing, in my new life, with things that really matter."

It felt like she was diving into deep, cold, dark water, not knowing what she would find; then discovering the joy of reaching out, plunging her arms in arcing strokes, kicking her legs, weightless and swimming.

The clock ticked an agonising beat.

Sophie glanced back into the room, beckoned by the rippled rivers of tinsel and spheres of glittering glass.

As an after-thought she added, "Merry Christmas, Mark," before firmly closing the door on his retreating back.

––––––––––

Published in *Baubles*, November 2016, Bridge House.

Glitter Globe Wedding

"There is a crack in everything, that's how the light gets in."

Leonard Cohen

"Good becomes perfect, but perfect is an illusion. And illusions are like all spells-temporary and soon broken. And when that happens, feelings change."

Erin McCahan

The smooth, cool sides curled into the palm of her hand. She only had to tilt it slightly to see the glitter dust descend.

Inside the glass ball stood a woman in a mauve gown, with her hands snugly tucked into a soft grey muff. Posed next to her was a straight backed man in a navy suit, with high golden buttons.

The more she shook their world, the more beautiful it became, as iridescent crystals fluttered in the air and flittered across trees, before settling into silver mounds. She loved whirring the glistening pieces around, whilst the figurines remained unmoved.

Then one day she shook it too vigorously and dropped the glass ball, which clattered and rolled across the wooden floor. It only made a crack, but little by little the water and glimmering glitter seeped out.

Now the couple stood raw, exposed, with clumsily painted smiles on their faces. The tree froze, rigid and plastic, its arms raised in outrage. The overarching sky was an empty, hollow dome. No shimmer, no shine; no magic will return the opalescent globe into a sparkling sphere.

She knew that she could never look at her Glitter Ball world the same way again.

The Wild Ones

"There is no passion to be found playing small – in settling for a life that is less than the one you are capable of living."

Nelson Mandela

"Drawing is not what you see but what you must make others see."

Edgar Degas

They say, "Don't play with fire," but what happens when the trouble is not of our making? That the simple act of being born is enough to stir up the deepest, darkest hatred?

The worst kind of enemy to have is the one that is sensed, but unseen. True I had attracted hostility before, particularly from some women, but this was something more dangerous. More pungent, bitter and potent; a hatred engrained like a cavernous scar that both hurt its owner and was part of them.

Some evenings as I trudged home through the dusky trees I would almost feel it like a force, radiating towards me through the pale beams of light. Then I would shudder, shrug and stride on, only more rapidly.

Yet the feeling would remain.

I lived with my grandmother. In fact I don't recall my mother as she died shortly after I was born. Nor would anyone speak of her other than to say that I had inherited her glossy black hair and her dark emerald green eyes. And her gift.

I smiled with relief as I reached the remote cottage, which was cosily wrapped up in a blanket of trees. I entered my grandmother's kitchen and inhaled as steam wafted upwards from a pot bubbling on the stove.

My grandmother turned her flushed, lovely face towards me. "What is wrong Cara? You look troubled." Her watery blue eyes scanned my face.

"I had that feeling again. Of being watched by someone or something malevolent. Only each time it happens it gets worse. This time I sensed the poisonous spite so deeply, it felt like bile in my throat."

My grandmother turned back to her pot without a word, keen not to betray any emotion. But I saw the crease between her brow and the set of her mouth and I knew. I felt her fear.

A moment elapsed. A steadying of breath. Then she murmured, "This is the time to harness your gift Cara. Use it now. Like your life depends on it."

I sat on the stool by the fire, fingering the discarded tassels of my grandmother's shawl.

"How do I do that?" I whispered.

"By keeping your mind clear. Don't lose your focus, never forget your visions and you must not fall too deeply in love," she replied vehemently.

I let the silky folds fall between my fingers. Unbidden I saw him. The slightly wild black hair and wry grin. The man I'd never met who seemed to taunt me with his dark, dangerous eyes.

There had been lads at school that I had passed time with. But none of them had ever really reached me.

"What happened to my mother?" I blurted.

My grandmother sharply jerked her face in my direction. "She fell in love with a Wild One, your father," she muttered. "They became lost in each other; they grew careless, like one lost soul. They didn't see the dangers. And then…"

"What?" I breathed.

My grandmother thumped the saucepan off the stove.

All I could see was her stooped head as she scraped it with a wooden spoon.

"Please. I need to know!" I begged.

"No," she replied with pursed lips. "There are some things that you're better off not knowing."

"Then how can I protect myself?" I cried exasperated. "How can I stop myself from making the same mistakes?"

Even as I spoke I knew that my plea was useless. I saw the stubborn fold of her arms before she whisked off her apron and draped it on the chair.

"It's enough to know that it killed both your parents. Follow the three Silver Rules and by that light let it guide your life."

Wearily I nodded. "Yes, yes I know. Forge my own path, don't follow another's. Treat others as I'd like to be treated. Value what I have instead of craving what I lack."

I had been reciting the Silver Rules since I was three, so much so that they had become the meaningless chant of a nursery rhyme. But my grandmother looked pleased as she nodded her head.

I remembered them again that night as I lay huddled in my bed. The wind was whipping the trees outside and sending a chill breeze down my chimney. I wrapped my blankets tightly around me, so that finally my body relaxed and I seeped into a strange, restless sleep. Once again I saw him. He was walking with swift, muscular movements and I was racing behind, struggling to keep up. Then abruptly he turned. His dark eyes stared directly into mine, deeper and deeper as though he could see my very soul. I opened my mouth to speak, but no sound came out. Then with a jolt I awoke.

I lay in bed panting, afraid and not knowing why my heart beat wildly. My head felt like it was spinning.

Then out of the darkness I felt it; a volcanic lava of red hot dislike. My palms burned, my whole body was covered in sweat. For a moment I stopped breathing, shaken to my core by such intense dislike.

I do not know how long I lay like that, but eventually I saw the soft syrupy light of dawn filter through my curtains and with it a slow relief. Gradually my heart beat returned to a regular rhythm and I unclenched my palms.

Resolutely I threw back my covers and hauled my clammy body to the shower. The calming water sparkled and tingled my skin. With fervour I washed away last night's fears in an aroma of oil and frothy bubbles.

I let my hair dry in front of the stove. I combed it through with some of my grandmother's special oil.

"I've decided to try that new gallery in the harbour," I murmured into my hair. "I've parcelled up a selection of my paintings so that they can see my range and I'll see what they have to say."

My grandmother straightened up after stoking the stove and she beamed at me.

"They can only reject me." I shrugged although inside I felt anything but glib. The thought of exposing my work to strangers turned my stomach, but we needed the money, so I had to take more of a commercial view.

My grandmother nodded. "A great idea, Cara."

I bundled my canvases into the boot of my car, all the while trying to instil some confidence into myself. Everyone who had seen my paintings had complimented me upon my talent. Even my Art teacher had commented upon the brilliancy of my craftsmanship.

The gallery was light and airy, with high arches and a pale grey stone floor. I expected to see what I had patronisingly termed, "seaside art", the usual mementos aimed at holidaymakers. So I was not prepared for the impact that the paintings had on me, their depth or their passion. I walked around each picture, sometimes captivated by a small detail, like a doe-eyed donkey braying, at other times a tear stained child's face pulled me in.

Then I stopped abruptly. My attention was arrested by a statue of a naked woman. There was nothing smooth and serene about it, no soft features or gentle curves. Every line in its angular body held hatred. Its malevolent face was screwed up with such intense dislike that I felt that at any moment it would come spitting into life, its hair thrashing like serpents.

I was so horror struck by this creature that I had no awareness of anyone else in the gallery.

A cool male voice behind me made my heart stop. "She's rather vivid isn't she?" He sounded amused. "A self-sculpture would you believe?"

I swung around and my throat dried. My lips parted, but I could not speak, for facing me was the dark haired man in my fantasies. *How can it be?* I wondered. *This simply isn't possible.*

His eyes seemed to glint with amusement, but I saw too that he was appraising me. I felt intensely uneasy.

"The artist's name is Sharika and she's remarkably talented. It's not always comfortable to look at, but then art should take you to unexplored places within yourself, don't you think?"

Again that searching look that left me feeling so lost, so young.

"So what brings you to the Moon Gallery?" Once more he took charge of the situation and I saw him glance at my bundles.

I took a deep breath. "I was hoping to speak to the gallery owner," I offered. "I've got some paintings I'd like to show." My voice trailed off and I felt vulnerable, rooted to the spot. Somehow those dark eyes seemed to see right through me.

"That'll be me then." He grinned and he really had the most kissable looking mouth. I tore my eyes away as he held out his hand for me to shake. "I'm Paul, the proprietor of Moon Gallery. Why don't you spread your canvases out along the counter here and I'll have a look at them."

Long moments passed as he peered at each and every one. I saw him frown as though he was thinking deeply.

Eventually, after what felt like a life-time, he straightened up. "Well technically they're very good," he said.

"But," I added, my heart fluttered waiting for the final hammer blow.

"But they're not inspirational."

I gasped. I could feel my cheeks redden. No-one had ever criticised my work before. He gauged my reaction, but continued, as though reading my mind.

"I'm sure everyone you know has told you how good you are. And as schoolgirl art this is excellent."

"Schoolgirl art!" I could feel the pulsing of anger and I was glad.

"I didn't mean to upset you," he said with the kind of wry smile which showed that he knew exactly the impact his words would have, "but this kind of stuff comes along all the time."

"Stuff!" I spluttered.

"Well you know, painting by numbers art, where the artist just paints what they see."

"What other kind is there?" I sprung around with irritation, yet I had to know the answer.

"Well there's art as it is perceived, felt, experienced. I think perhaps you're too young to have felt any intense emotions and so you cannot channel them into your art."

"I'm nineteen!" I threw back at him and only just resisted the urge to stamp my foot.

"Exactly," he agreed. Then almost under his breath he

added, "But you will. Soon, sooner than you realise." He shrugged. "Enjoy the calm."

"Whatever do you mean?" I felt as though fireworks were exploding in my head.

He looked directly at me as though accepting a challenge and I felt pinned to the spot by those deep dark eyes.

Almost as though he was changing the subject he gestured for me to stand beside him as we looked at my paintings.

"Look what do you see?" he asked.

I shrugged. "Waves, a beach, seagulls."

"But what are they doing?" he persisted. "Where is the movement, the mood? Everything is in its place, but painted without passion." I felt his arm sweep against mine as he circled the motion of a wave.

He turned to face me directly, so closely that I could feel his breath. "Go back," he whispered. "Go back and look. Feel. Forget your technical skills. Be there. Paint from your inner being. Ignore everything you've been taught, and see with your soul." He placed his hands on my shoulders. Crazily, annoyingly I could feel my heart pounding.

"Then," he murmured as I sank into his gaze, "then come back and show me."

I was spellbound so I had not heard her light footsteps. It was only when a voice like splintered glass broke into the moment that Paul released his hands from my shoulders, briefly brushing them against my arms.

"More amateur stuff." She laughed, her golden hair thrown back in disdain. Her grey eyes narrowed as she took me in, then dismissively, as though throwing a handful of dust she added, "Careful Paul, or you'll be the object of yet another schoolgirl crush."

Paul's eyes narrowed. "This is Sharika," he said unnecessarily. For it was clear that in spite of her beauty, she was the sculptor of the statue.

"Her talent is rare," he added, yet his tone seemed to suggest something more, less reverential and more threatening.

I nodded and clumsily bundled my canvases together, all the while aware that I was being scrutinised by two sets of eyes.

The stone floor space to the exit felt long as I scurried to leave. Somehow my humiliation felt worse for Sharika's knowing grin.

Yet as I reached the door Paul threw out, "You are the daughter of Marie and John Grove aren't you?" I bolted around and stared straight at him. It was not a question, more of an observation.

In angry defiance I lifted my chin. "They're my parents, both dead now."

He nodded unimpressed. "Both Wild Ones too."

I let the door swing shut behind me, but not before I had seen the look on Sharika's face. *What did he mean by 'too'?*

By the time I had reached my grandmother's I was flaming with fury. This only increased in the light of her composure as I recounted the tale.

"You're still young," she almost whispered, "and there's still so much for you to learn."

"You mean I should try to be more like that Sharika, all twisted emotions!"

"I mean that you should forge your own path," she added gently, then shuddered. "Sharika, I think I know that name, but I can't fathom why. Perhaps if she's very talented I've seen her work exhibited somewhere."

I shrugged.

"Clearly she can make an impact," she commented.

In spite of myself I found Paul's words spinning around my head. I wanted to hit out. *Why is he such an expert? Surely I could take my pictures to one of the bigger retailers on the coast and they would find a place for them. Why is he so knowledgeable? He can only be a few years older than me.*

For a few days I alternated between moping and stomping around the countryside. I was restless and I could not settle. No matter where I went or what I did I kept seeing his face. Worse still, in spite of my humiliation I wanted, almost needed to see him again.

Eventually I grabbed a couple of clean canvases with my brushes and paints, to set off for Needles Point with a spectacular view on a cliff edge. I let my anger take hold. With swirling brush strokes I arched the curve of waves as the sea came crashing to the shore, flailing its spray in all directions.

Time passed and I managed to capture a fiery sunset which burned on the horizon and glazed the sea in a burning light.

Exhilarated I lifted up my canvas and placed it next to my bag; I did not want to stay late, but I was keen to capture the early fingers of shade hovering over the sea.

A gull flew towards me and swooped over my painting, giving a whirring cry. In my head the screeching seemed to get louder and shriller, vibrating across the sea in harsh alarm. My palms grew sweaty, my breathing shallow, yet still my feet remained rooted to the spot.

I dared not turn around. Like deep green snake poison I felt the hatred bore into me. The wind hissed through my hair and my heart missed a beat.

In one swift movement I leapt aside. I shrieked. A boulder whirled past me ripping my painting off its stand and sending it plummeting down the cliff below. I watched as it spun in a grotesque dance, whirling and twirling before being engulfed by the angry sea.

That could have been me.

Slowly I turned. Nothing. Only a flicker of a shadow between some trees.

I shuddered. *If I had not moved at that moment I would be dead by now. Yet if it had been a mini avalanche of rocks, surely I would have heard it. All of the stones were still. How could one rock move like that through the air on its own? Surely it would be too big for one person to heave?*

I turned again to stare at the pine woodland behind me. Had I detected a movement in the charcoal gaps between the trees? The more I tried to fathom their depths, the more convinced I became that I was being watched.

The cawing of a crow brought me back to the sea. Slowly I edged my feet forward towards my bag, paints and remaining canvas. I had to retrieve these. I knew that my finished painting was unlike anything I had ever done before. That I had poured into it my anger, my yearning.

I crouched down as I neared the rocks; I hated feeling such a visible target. Loose pebbles dislodged under my feet as I reached forward. My hand seized the strap of my bag and I swung it behind me. Next I must grab the canvas.

Once again I glanced towards the darkening woodland. The trees seemed more bunched together, threatening. I knew that I had to act quickly as the shadowy darkness seeped into the coastland. With a final wrench I leant forward and retrieved my painting. All that remained was my stand, which hung limply further down the rocks as though on a hangman's gibbet. That I would have to leave.

The dark trees stood like sentries warning me not to enter. The fir cones were soft and spongy under foot, yet every now and then my foot snapped a twig which seemed to echo like gun fire in the waiting woodland. All the while I knew I was being watched, as though the place was pulsing with another heartbeat. Each step seemed to match mine, but another echo was striking up as though someone was secretly trailing me. I stood still, my heart beating wildly. The woodland seemed to hold its breath too, waiting for my next move. And I knew that someone else was there with me. Someone who wanted to remain hidden.

When I finally pushed open my grandmother's door I could feel my hands shaking. Soft light from the kitchen spilled out into the forest, bathing it in a greenish glow.

She smiled, as always pleased to see me. "Two things before I forget," she said as she rose to fill the kettle. "Remember that I've got my hospital visit on Tuesday."

I had not forgotten, but she patted my cheek reassuringly at the concern on my face. "Nothing to worry about," she added. "Now what was the other thing?" she pondered as she pulled out two cups. "Oh yes, you had a visitor."

"A visitor?" I echoed. Somehow I just knew that it was not a school friend.

"Yes." She surveyed me keenly. "Dark hair and eyes, very good looking in an untamed kind of way. He asked where he might find you. It seemed kind of urgent, so I told him that you would probably be painting at the cliff edge at Needles Point. Did he find you?"

"Yes, um no, I don't think so," I faltered. How did Paul know where I lived? How for that matter did he know my parents' names? I took my tea upstairs as there were so many things I had to think through. *What exactly did he mean when he said, "They were Wild Ones too?" None of this made any sense.*

Most frightening and threatening of all, why did I always feel myself to be in danger when my thoughts turned to him? It all seemed so ridiculous. If I told anyone they would just think me crazy. The only person I could share it with was my grandmother and there was no way I could burden her with more worry before she went into hospital.

That night I slept deeply until the first pale light of dawn. Then my head had the sensation of spinning, swirling out of control. Plunging and plummeting into a pool of darkness. The dense black vortex pulled me in, spinning me around as though in some deadly black hole. Deeper and darker I sunk as my pale limbs spun like turbines out of control. My eye lids felt heavy as though pennies had been laid over them, the way they rest corpses. With an effort I wrenched them open. Slowly the shadowy room stopped spinning. It took a moment to work out where I was. A terrible chill seeped into the room and the bed covers fluttered.

It was just my over active imagination I told myself. The result of wandering around at dusk. I stretched and turned on my side, ready to return to sleep. Then I saw it: my window flapping open.

I knew that I had not left it that way, not in my current frame of mind. Perhaps my grandmother had decided to air the room and forgotten to close it properly? It might have been wrenched open by a gust of wind? I leapt up to close it and stared out into the inky blackness. I knew that I was being watched. I sensed movement. I felt a presence.

Somehow I must have slept again, for I was awoken by a shrill wind and the crackle of rain, like tiny pebbles being thrown against my window.

"I'm going to stay inside to paint today," I announced to Gran, glad of an excuse to remain inside the warmth of her cottage. "I'm afraid I'll have to balance a couple of stools for an easel though."

"Why?" my grandmother looked at me quizzically. "Your easel is in the porch where you left it."

I counted a missed heartbeat, then smiled. Whatever happens, I thought, I must not tell her a thing. She does not need to worry about me.

Leaning against the sturdy stone wall stood my easel. The only signs of its adventure were a splash of red paint, a scrape down one side and a tiny piece of gravel in a groove. Looped over one leg spun a sliver of silver ribbon. I pulled it off and wound it around my wrist. It was odd, but I wanted to wear it.

This time my painting showed a platinum dawn sky. The shimmering silver sea hung back expectantly waiting as faint tendrils of light lit the gentle ripples It was full of joyful anticipation as though holding its breath.

Now I am ready I thought as I drove my grandmother to hospital along the winding lanes. Now I must meet Paul with my pictures.

First I made my grandmother as comfortable as I could in her ward bed. As I turned down the covers and filled a bowl with fruit I could feel my stomach flipping over. Of course I was concerned for her, but soon she gave me her slow smile. "Stop fussing Cara and get on with all your chores. If you hang around here much longer that gallery will close."

I nodded. Butterflies were twisting around in my stomach as I walked away. All my security had vanished in a moment.

The gallery door was shut, but it yielded open with a push. No-one was in sight. My eyes became drawn to a painting, a swirling vortex of passion, sinister in its dark colours, which pulled the viewer in like the centre of the storm. I felt as though I was drowning and I realised that I had stopped breathing.

"That's Sharika's. Her talent is truly phenomenal."

Once more I spun around at his voice. Why is it that I never hear him enter?

For a moment I could not look up at him. All I felt was a bilious moment of envy. To be Sharika, to hold that much talent, to have the power and passion to impress Paul.

95

Then I remembered the Silver Rules. I must forge my own way, not copy or envy others. Only then did I raise my eyes and meet Paul's.

He gave a half smile as though he could read my thoughts. "So what have you brought in?" he asked gently, as though to a child.

Defensively I clutched my paintings closer. I was not ready yet to feel so exposed, so vulnerable.

I raised my chin in challenge. "Have you been to Needles Point recently?" I allowed him to see the silver ribbon around my wrist.

The shimmer caught his eyes before they travelled to my face. "Yes," was the bald reply.

I swayed from foot to foot, already out of my depth. Then with surging trepidation I placed the bundles before him.

I watched his long, slim fingers as he tenderly unwrapped the cotton sheets around my canvases. His arms looked strong as he held the first one up. He nodded. It was enough. Gently he placed it back on the counter before slipping his fingers through the soft white cotton surrounding the second canvas.

"We'll call this one Anticipation," he said with a slow smile. "The calm before the storm, the moment when you hold your breath before giving way to passion."

He moved closer to me, to sweep back my hair from my face. "You're starting to shine," he whispered. I felt the light touch of his fingers against my cheeks and I closed my eyes. His warm body moved closer so that his next words were so near my lips they were almost a kiss, "No, I mustn't. It's too dangerous."

Stung I cried back, "I'm not a schoolgirl now you know!"

"I know," he agreed ruefully. "That's the problem. Be careful."

I drew away. "Why is everyone telling me to be careful? And from what?"

"Use the Silver Rules as your shield. All Wild Ones have a special talent, sometimes that can help too."

"A special talent?" I queried.

"Yes everyone has something. But as a Wild One all of your abilities and qualities can become more developed or even extreme. So if for example your particular gift is compassion for others, well as a Wild One it becomes more so."

"So what if," I looked speculatively at him, "what if someone felt a really negative emotion, like anger, or envy or," I hesitated afraid to even say it, "hatred."

He looked back at me with mesmerising dark eyes, but his face went blank, giving nothing away. "Then they'd feel hatred, only more so. It would be deeper, darker, more deadly."

I gasped like I had been kicked in the stomach. "But the Silver Rules…"

"The Silver Rules give some protection, not always enough. They shield people from themselves, so if followed they can stop a Wild One being destroyed by their own negative passions."

"How do you know all of this?"

"Isn't it obvious?" With a sharp flick he opened a notepad.

Once again I had that hollow sensation in my stomach. "So you're a Wild One too."

Paul gave a barely discernible nod of his head and passed me a piece of paper. "I've written down the prices that I think we'll get for your two pictures, but we'll have to wait and see. In the meantime I look forward to some more."

I nodded, disappointed now to be walking away. I leant

over to refasten my bag, hoping somehow to delay the moment. Then I felt it, like a sharp needle jutting into my side, burning with fierce angry intensity. The side of my face felt gauged, scraped by sharp, vicious claws.

This can't be happening, I thought. Not here. Not now. With Paul looking down at me, with an expression full of what?

Suddenly he seized my arm and swung me close towards him. At that moment Sharika's life sized model toppled to the place where I had just stood. Its angry limbs and flailing hair smashed like a clap of thunder on to the floor.

Neither of us moved for a moment. I could feel Paul's arms holding me close, away from the grotesque, misshapen creature that lay in splattered shards across the floor.

Yet surely we were the only ones in the gallery? Who else but Paul could have toppled it over?

"Sharika." I shuddered as though the body of the real woman lay in front of me.

Paul frowned. "You two may have more in common than you realise," he commented. "You both lost your mothers when you were very young." Then almost as an afterthought, "You're both Wild Ones."

And we may have fallen for the same person? The wrong man?

Paul spoke into my hair, "It is terrible to see talent destroy itself." Then gently he placed my bag on my shoulder and led me towards the door.

I was still pondering over his enigmatic words, when he added like a punch in the ribs, "Keep away from cliff tops."

So he knew.

That night I felt intensely, miserably alone. I knew that my grandmother would only be away for two more days, but I missed her gentle comforting presence.

I tried to piece it all together. Did the gallery bring the Wild Ones together? Perhaps it helped to have an artistic outlet for intense passions?

My head whirled with stormy emotions. Everything seemed to revolve around the gallery and in the centre, the eye of the storm, there was Paul. I could not help being drawn towards him, yet I knew nothing, absolutely nothing about him, except that he is a Wild One and that seemed like a very dangerous knowledge.

I knew that I was on the brink of something potent, frightening and exciting. I also felt like it had a momentum of its own, like falling off a cliff. I must be wary after my parents' fate. My Wild Ones gift gives me a warning of danger and I must heed it now as it is all I have to save me.

But some forces are too powerful to be resisted.

The evening began gently enough. I warmed up a tomato soup. Then as I felt the chill stirring of the wind in the eaves, I went outside to collect some logs from the outhouse. Long evening shadows slid around the cottage. I looked up at the early moon which stood out sharp and clear. The woodland seemed strangely still and silent, as though holding its breath.

I bundled the logs into my arms and lifted the latch to the back door. Tonight I decided I would leave nothing to chance. Every door and window would be locked and bolted. I pushed my weight against the door; it was secure and sturdy. Even the thick stone walls of the cottage offered reassurance.

I found comfort in wrapping my grandmother's soft, silky shawl around my arms and imagining her presence.

I suppose I must have dozed like that, for I do not recall anything until I was jolted by the screeching whine of the wind down the chimney. The window frames shook and the door latch was knocking, although I knew no-one would choose to be out on an evening like this.

Again and again I heard the banging on the door, the insistent pounding like a fist demanding entry. Surely the knocker was too heavy to be lifted by the wind?

Uneasily I stoked the fire, trying to block out the hammering sound that was rebounding around my head. No wind could make this much noise. But this was no normal night.

Then I felt my chest tightening and the welling up of absolute fear. I knew that this was the moment. My head throbbed with the thumping on the door and this became the rhythm of my heart beat. My blood pounded and all the while I heard the wild wailing of the wind whirling around the cottage.

I knew what I had to do. My knees felt weak. The banging became louder and louder, exploding inside my head. I forced myself forward, with one hesitant step in front of the other, towards the door.

I could not keep it out, or control it. The fire leapt in the grate as I began to draw back the heavy bolt. The knocking stopped. Silence. Slowly I lifted the latch. The door wrestled itself from my grasp as it flung itself open.

I almost fell onto the path outside. A high pitched screech echoed through the woodland, the sound of a predator killing its prey. Pine cones and leaves were flung up from the ground and thrown against my face, temporarily blinding my vision. I felt as though claws were tearing at my body. A cold, intense hatred bit into my spine like the chill of being punctured by a dozen icicles.

Still I stepped forward. It was then that I felt a sense of urgency. I ran with my heart pounding and without looking back at the flapping door. I had to reach Needle Point, fast. Trees clawed at my clothes, but I wrestled my way through, deeper and darker into the woodland. The shadowy pine trees seemed to block out the force of the wind and the sea, almost deadly in their silence.

My side felt raw from running, but still I plunged on. It was crazy, but as I did so I understood that love and reason do not work together. Some force, greater than my own survival was pulling me.

I flung myself out into the clearing, my breath ragged, my sides burning. A flash of dry lightning lit up the sky, but there was still no answering thunder or rain. Waves thrashed against the Needle rocks, but at first glance the scene seemed empty. Forward I ran without thought or caution.

Then I stopped. I froze, rooted to the spot. For there in front of me, as still and as motionless as a black rock, stood Paul.

I gasped. His face showed anguish. Was he the threat that I was trying to confront? Was this a battle of wills against myself?

"Cara!" he called, his voice hurled against the waves. "Go now, before it's too late!"

I swung around. A zigzag snake of lightning flared against a rock. There she stood, her golden hair burning around a face boiling with loathing. I could not move against the force of her hated.

Sharika stepped forward. A slow grin etched jagged lines across her face, carved from years of bitterness.

"At last," she hissed. "You have no idea how long I've waited for this moment."

Paul stretched out an arm, but she laughed. Nothing could stop her now.

"I must thank you," she gleamed up at him, "for bringing her to me."

I looked at him. Had Paul been part of this scheme? Did he intend to feed me to her, like a mouse to a rattlesnake?

He stood motionless, his muscles flexed, showing no emotion. I tried to do the same.

Sharika grinned, her sharp eyes boring into mine. Her legs were astride, her frizzy hair parted like a tarantula's legs.

She drew closer to me and in almost hypnotic undertones murmured, "I feel your fear. I will crush your spirit and watch your insides wither. The greater your pain, the happier it makes me. You're just like your mother."

This stung me into alertness. "You knew my mother!"

Sharika dismissed her. "Only briefly as a child. You could say my mother knew her very well indeed. Then there's your father; my mother knew him first. He should never have left her. A fatal mistake. They deserved to die."

Furiously I hurtled towards her, my anger pulled me beyond thought. In a moment Paul was at my side, caging my arms. "The Silver Rules," he whispered, "be true to yourself."

I lost sight of Sharika as thunder echoed around the cliffs and forks of lightning flashed between the trees.

"And now you!" she spat, her voice hurled between boulders of rocks.

"Watch out!" Paul yelled as he hurled me to one side. A rock came crashing towards us. Further flints and stones came raining down upon us, yet somehow Paul managed to deflect them and pull me to safety. So his Wild Ones' gift was hidden strength. Even so, nothing could be a match against Sharika's engrained hatred.

"We can't stand exposed on this boulder!" Paul yelled. "Try to move downwards to the rocks below, then we'll gain some cover."

There was another momentous clap of thunder and then the rain fell, in great crashing torrents, stinging our eyes. We edged away from the cliff drop, all the while aware of the treacherously slippery surface.

I shuddered. "It's a long drop!"

"Be careful!" Paul cautioned. "The rocks are like daggers and the pools are deep."

As dark and deep as death I thought as I scuttled around a coffin shaped boulder.

"Move aside!" I called as Paul managed to adroitly miss the curve of another missile.

"It's not much further," Paul gave an encouraging glance. "Just watch you don't slip in this rain."

Almost in slow motion, the small stones beneath our feet started sliding. As they did so they churned up bigger rocks and boulders, so that we were caught up in a massive, heaving avalanche.

I screamed. Paul was swung away from me and winded as he took a glancing blow in the stomach from a rock. I was flung upwards across the stones, like a kite helplessly flapping in the wind. Down I swept faster and faster. My nails scrabbled to cling to passing boulders, which scratched and stung.

At that moment Sharika bowled a stone beneath me which dislodged my feet and sent me sliding out of control. My arms flailed wildly as I shrieked and the air seemed to be filled with screaming. The sea pool rose to meet me and I became engulfed in stinging salty water.

A green mist of hatred flooded chokingly into my lungs. Deeper I sunk and deeper, away from sight or sound. Even as I floundered I knew that this was how my parents had died.

With a wild, desperate kick I heaved my body to the surface. I seized one gasping lungful of air before being pulled downwards again.

I felt a threat above me, but I could not be sure of its direction. I saw a white arm reaching out, the fingers spread like grasping tentacles. But whose? Could it be Sharika waiting to push me under or hurl me against a rock?

Blindly I threw out both arms and felt a firm grasp. Water rushed around my body as I was heaved towards the rocks. I felt the scrape of the harsh surface as I coughed and spluttered. A hand lifted me up and steadied my gasping body. I nestled into Paul as he held me close. Tenderly he stroked my back until my breathing steadied.

My lungs were raw and sore. "Sharika?" I gasped. "Where is she?"

"Your parents were Wild Ones which meant that their dying wish became a sacred covenant," Paul whispered. "That deep love would overcome bitter hatred."

I followed his gaze to the edge of the forest. Jagged forks of lightning lit the pines in a silvery light. At first I thought I saw a blackened tree split by lightning. Then I recognised the distorted frozen form.

"Sharika was torn apart by her own hatred," Paul explained. "She had such talent, but her anger ate away at her inside."

I shivered uncontrollably. Paul wrapped me in his arms and lifted me up. "When we were in danger we called to each other without realising it." The rain had flattened his hair and was running down his face in rivulets. "I was worried though, so terrified that I might lose you."

He cupped my face in his hands and kissed me. I threw my arms around his neck and pulled him closer. I forgot to breathe. My head spun.

Paul smiled at me with such tenderness. "Let's get you warm and dry in the cottage," he murmured. I nuzzled my head into his neck. With a smile he added, "Then we can really find out what it's like to be a Wild One."

Published in *Devils, Demons and Werewolves*, October 2010, Bridge House.

Bland New World

"Without passion man is a mere latent force and possibility, like the flint which awaits the shock of the iron before it can give forth its spark."

Henri Frederic Amiel

Ours is a world with the sharp edges polished off; as smooth and as round as a sea pebble.

How strange to think that only one hundred years ago life was as rough and jagged as one of their books. Yet I find myself riveted, as I once again become drawn to the diary entry. It is so odd that the pain and lack of symmetry radiating from the pages should pull me in, all the things that our society has erased.

I nearly stumbled in the fading light, but I didn't care. My heart was thumping in my ears as I clattered along the pavement. I kicked the loose stone out of my way and stubbed my foot, I was so angry.

Due to strict health and safety regulations, all pavements are padded and provided with proper illumination.

Yet another blazing row with my sister. I hate her smug smile! I hate the way she keeps taking my things! I hate her!

Although we are all single children, (as multiple breeding is not permitted,) we refer to each other as sister or brother. We all conform to a standard look of idealised beauty. There is no rivalry. Consequently we are all wrapped in a cotton wool contentment.

She gave that silly superior grin that she has, then went on and on about my low grades. Our parents have never forgiven me for dropping out of university and she loves to rub it in because she knows it annoys me.

We enjoy a virtual classroom environment with attainable

targets and no recriminations. We are all respected in equal measure.

I hadn't realised where I was running to that night. I was nowhere near my home. I was nowhere near my friends. I had no idea how much my life was going to change.

All of our social interactions must be positive, so they tend to be on the portable net. I am fortunate that I have a number of virtual friends, all of whom endorse my positive self-image. We meet on cyber play dates displayed on multi-dimensional screens. No-one ever feels lonely.

My only thought as I crashed through the door of the Red Lion was of the anger pumping through my veins.

For the mind we benefit from core centralisation. If a negative emotion impinges on our rational thought we can literally whisk it away until our central balance has been restored.

Muscle relaxants are used to dissipate any tension from our bodies.

There he was, nonchalantly leaning with his back against the wall, as though he didn't care about anything, although I knew that wasn't true.

I grabbed a chair nearest to the door. How many years ago was it that we last met? It must be at least five. But I'd know him anywhere. The way he slouched into his leather jacket and just let his clothes hang off him. The way his hair kept drooping across his forehead, the curve of his nose, with his slightly crooked smile. And I loved every part of him.

Due to prettification we are now all entitled to surgical enhancement. We are all identically, symmetrically beautiful. An affinity has filtered through society as we all look so similar to each other.

I allow myself a second to look between the shoulders

106

of the other drinkers. I fix my gaze upon him and I take a gulp. My once childhood friend, older and always looked up to, my first real crush.

Then there was that moment. His eyes flicked in my direction and I felt the flash of recognition. My heart stopped beating. Slowly his smile spread across his face and he sloped towards me. I wished that I didn't look such a mess.

I remained clenched to my chair, unable to breathe.

An image adjustor helps us to regulate our self-perception with actuality.

At first, all I was aware of was the exhilaration and the blur of the shadowy landscape, as we flew along on his motorbike. Roaring with power we sped along the lanes, making the countryside our own. I pressed closer to his back and nuzzled my face against his neck. He smelt of shampoo. I felt a surge of anticipation, knowing that when we stopped we would kiss.

We are in such self-contained units now that we have little need for transportation. When we do, we climb into a Link Compartment which is constructed like beads on a necklace. Providing we press the right buttons, we reach our destination at incredible speed.

He was late. The rain streamed down in a metallic grey curtain. It seemed to splutter and spurt onto every surface.

I paced the room. Waiting. The only sound was of the incessant drum beat of the rain as it thrashed on the roof.

There must be a reason. I checked my phone. He has not called. I tried again. Answer phone.

Still the rain hammered down.

We have temperature and meteorological regulators which ensure that we never have to face any adverse weather conditions. Consequently we often have a gentle shower of rain at around four in the morning.

I could not wait any longer. I rounded the corner in the direction of his house. Black iridescent puddles of oil seeped across the road.

Sharp jagged edges of metal leaned against the wall. A road sign drooped in a crooked curve.

I didn't hear the screeching brakes. The sharp intake of breath. The clunk of splintering metal. Sirens.

Only the silence and the splattering rain.

I noticed the words were smeared on the page, as though by rain. My own eyes felt as hard as marbles.

I got a paper cut from the page and a speck of blood dropped down.

For the first time ever I wanted to experience tears, not from my emotions, but from the lack of them.

———————————

Published in CaféLit Magazine, March 2022

Take Flight

"When everything seems to be going against you, remember that the airplane takes off against the wind, not with it."

Henry Ford

Chloe lifted the belt clip and eased into her seat with a sigh. Although the plane wheels had not even begun to taxi along the runway, she felt as though she had already been on a long journey.

Once more she saw herself standing in a pool of her long, silky dress which shimmered in aquamarine folds at her feet. She had taken great care with her appearance, her make-up, and jewellery. Her golden hair was softly coiled around the top of her head. She took a last glance at her reflection in the mirror and felt a shiver of excitement. For once she felt great as she lightly skipped down the stairs.

Bob glanced at his watch. "Come on, if we don't hurry up we'll be late," and they slammed out of the house.

Still she kept smiling, for he could be taciturn and simply not show his feelings. Yet she felt punched in the stomach when she watched at the ease with which he slipped away from her, quickly absorbed in the milling group of people.

Chloe watched as he smiled, joked and charmed. He had once said that he never thought he needed to try with her, and she had read that as a positive sign that he felt comfortable with her. Uncertainly she hovered on the outside of the group, her dress fluttering around her ankles like timid wings.

Bob leaned forward and complimented a curvy brunette on how ravishing she was looking. Chloe's smile stretched brightly. The woman dipped her head to drink in his words.

Then confidingly she rested her hand on Chloe's arm and whispered, "Your husband is the most marvellous man. Truly I don't know what the company would do without him. He is always so kind and gracious, a real gentleman." Still Chloe smiled as she hugged herself tightly.

Bob was, she knew, a perfectionist, and somehow she felt as though she never quite measured up. It was not so much the things he said, for he spoke little, but the contemptuous curl of his lips that he used so often when he bothered to evaluate her.

There were times when she tried to reach out, to trust. Once she even showed him a painting she had done. He handed it back to her without saying a single word. No further comment was ever made, just the stony gaze a schoolmaster would give a recalcitrant pupil for poor homework. She shrivelled up inside and stopped painting.

Chloe even tried dressing up for him, to try to become more alluring. Her heart fluttered frantically as she heard his footsteps on the stairs. She felt foolish in her black stockings and red basque. Bob's face reflected back at her, first blank, and then shocked as he said, "What are you doing?"

Chloe folded her arms around her body, longing to cover up. It reminded her of a childhood time when she had been severely reprimanded for smearing her mother's lipstick across her face. She was made to look at her face in the mirror, to see how foolish she had looked.

Perhaps Bob had not wanted to tell her how awful she looked? Certainly he showed contempt. After that he even considered her red, lacy knickers as being too racy, so she learned to dress more sedately.

Chloe began to realise that Bob was a man of secrets. He would disappear for long periods of time. At first it hurt when he vanished without so much as a goodbye or a peck on a cheek. She learned to shrug it off. Why should he account for his leisure hours to her? She was not his keeper. And she enjoyed slipping around the house alone, free to dream in her own little fantasy bubble.

But she noticed that money was slipping away. On the 5th of each month a chunk was removed from their bank account. He called it spread betting. He could not lose. He knew what he was doing. After all, what did she know about sport? She wouldn't understand.

Chloe hugged her arms closer around her body and squeezed her eyes shut.

The absences grew longer and longer, as she became increasingly alone. At strange hours she would receive phone calls, but the receiver would be abruptly slammed down when she answered the phone.

Chloe noticed that Bob took more trouble with his appearance. He bought new underwear, a strange aftershave. Whenever she questioned him he would sneer in contempt, leaving her feeling inadequate.

Their house started to deteriorate with neglect. Little things at first: a broken floor board, unkept lawn, faulty doorbell. Then they had a problem with the plumbing, but he refused to look into it or seek outside help. His clothes were strewn all over the floor and objects were just dumped in every room. Chloe did not like to nag, yet she found it increasingly difficult to hide herself away and relax. As it became ever more crowded with junk from Bob's numerous shopping sprees, she felt more and more enclosed and suffocated.

She found real comfort in food, particularly chocolate. For brief moments of bliss she would curl up with her snacks and her book, shutting out the other world. He observed her burgeoning waist line with a sneer, although no comment was spoken.

Some things would not be shut out, not even with the click of a switch. It was the internet which forced the outer world into Chloe's consciousness. At first it was not with exotic beaches and exciting travel tales, but watching Bob hastily switch websites when she stepped into the study. Initially she dismissed it, but it gnawed at the back of her mind.

One morning, when Bob got swept outside by a wild wind which whipped up stray leaves, she crept into his study. Chloe glanced nervously over her shoulder, then she logged on to Bob's website history: Big and Brassy, Bouncy Boobs, Voluptuous Beauties. She stared in horror as the naked truth was laid bare before her. He seemed so indifferent to her body, yet he stared at these. She felt sick.

Then as she clicked off the switch, anger rose within her. What had those women got that she had not?

Her blood burned. Chloe dug out the bank statements and made some phone calls. She boxed up her valuable items, those that were personal, with no shared history. She knew what she had to do.

With relief Chloe sank her head back against the plane seat. Her frenzied blood was no longer racing through her. She could relax.

Chloe stole one last look at her laptop before she stored it in the overhead locker. She imagined Bob switching on to the Voluptuous Beauties page as he did every evening at 6pm. His eyes would alight on her back with her long golden hair cascading over her body, hinting, but revealing nothing. Her head was turned sideways with an arch smile. She saw him casually scrolling along the women, his eyes dilating, then his expression as he leaned forward.

Like all of their communication, her message was curt and remote. Lastly he would read the simple words lipsticked across her back, "Bye Bob".

She snapped shut the laptop with finality. Chloe was carried now by the motion of events that she had put in place. She felt the wheels move beneath her, hurling her along the runway towards a new adventure. The nose lifted, reaching into the air. As the wings took flight Chloe felt that she too had her arms open once more as she reached out to life.

Published in *Going Places*, May 2010, Bridge House.

Wake Up Call

"We are not always what we seem, and hardly ever what we dream."

Peter Beagle

Once upon a time, in a land far away, there was a beautiful princess, who was as fair as fair can (unnaturally) be. She was as good as she was beautiful, which in case you were wondering, was very good indeed.

Her only problem was that she required an excessive amount of beauty sleep, one hundred years to be precise.

So, when the handsome prince in tight fitting breeches found her, she was enjoying a little shut eye.

One sight of her completely took his breath away. (To tell the truth he was also a tad breathless on account of having to hack his way through the undergrowth surrounding the castle, as a good gardener could not be found for love or money.) Which was almost as bad as wading through her massive shoe collection; in fact he nearly got himself impaled on one of her ruby slippers. But then a girl can never have too many pairs of shoes.

Anyway, to cut to the chase, the prince kissed her cherry red, perfect Cupid's bow lips. When she could get a word in edgeways, the princess opened her big Bambi eyes and said, "My Prince!" Which was perhaps a bit presumptuous and premature.

Notwithstanding, they married in haste in an intimate ceremony, with just a thousand or two honoured guests, some of whom they knew.

Certainly the blushing bride looked radiant at the side of her perfect prince, as she anticipated a life of wedded bliss in the happily ever after.

True, she had a problem or two with her mother-in-law, who would put a hard pea under the mattress of her bed and who gave her a glass slipper as a bit of a joke. She wasn't sure about all that stuff about talking to her reflection in the mirror either.

Even the prince appeared to have picked up one or two bad habits on the way. He certainly owned some beautiful things, but in her opinion he spent far too much time frantically rubbing on his magic lamp.

Of course he was entitled to own his ugly duckling and his share of furry friends, after all every dog must have his day; it was just that pushy little Puss in Boots that she couldn't stand.

Over time she began to realise that he wasn't everyone's cup of tea, particularly hers, but that there was no point in crying over spilt milk.

Nor could she really understand why the prince would insist upon climbing up her long flowing hair to reach their tower room, when there was a perfectly good spiral staircase.

On reaching the summit he would scratch his head and mutter, "I'm sure I came in here for something."

It was at that point that she realised that the perfect prince she had married had turned into a flipping frog.

The best that she could hope for was to wake up and discover that it had all been just a dream.

Published in *The Best of Café Lit 6*, August 2017, Chapeltown Books.

Anticipation

"Three may keep a secret, if two of them are dead."
Benjamin Franklin

Everyone has a secret. For some it's like a dirty, scrunched up piece of paper shoved into a back pocket, taken out and examined in quiet moments. Others bury them deep in the ground and pile up layers of rock on top.

My job is to unearth them, no matter how deeply they are hidden. Some might say that I'm a kind of confessor, granting absolution for their sins. I see myself as a dentist, rummaging around for festering, decaying matter and drilling it out. I don't fill the gap with silver though – that's what they give to me.

The skill is to create a sense of suspense and mystery. My caravan quietly slips onto the village green during the dark of the moon. A flickering candle in the window keeps me in the shadows, and when I look out, they just see the outlining of my deep kohl lined eyes. It's all window dressing of course, from the tasselled table cloth to the china tea set and the glaring black cat. I even wear a shawl edged with coins. They glint in the soft light as a reminder that I need paying.

At dawn I slink down the steps with a bag of cards that I distribute in the local cafes. Sometimes I will melt into the background near a group of women with children, listening. Plenty of secrets are spilt amongst the laughter and slopped milkshakes.

Later, as I pass by, I will hand them my fortune teller cards, make eye contact and smile. When I leave, I turn around, almost as an afterthought, a joke, and I say, "Bring your partners too. Who knows what guilty secrets they may be hiding?" It works.

116

Show time is between five and ten in the evening, with only one person admitted into my caravan for a private reading. That's very important. A sign displayed in my window shows whether they must wait or may enter. I see the feet and legs first, under the black doorway curtain as they climb up the steps, always slightly hesitant. By the time the curtain has been swept across, I have made my first assessment.

This time it's a man – tall, works out in a gym, dyed brown hair to hide his age, designer jeans. He stands in front of the curtain, fingers hooked into his pockets, legs spread wide. I stare, I don't move or speak, keeping him held on the spot and owning my space. It's not what he expects. He glances at the chair and shuffles his expensive trainers. Only then do I sweep a jangling arm to the seat opposite mine, ensuring that the coins shimmer in the candle light. He sits quickly, too fast, almost toppling the chair.

My smile is slow, languorous. I notice the way his glance sweeps my cleavage in the tight bodice, but my dark eyes look straight at him.

Instantly I flash out the cards tucked up my sleeve into a swirling peacock tail across the table, catch them up, sharply smack them into a pile and fan them out again.

There's a glint, a challenge in my eyes which I know he hasn't missed as I flick out a Tarot card. I turn it over and we see a fiery sky illuminating two naked bodies entwined, as they are partially submerged in water. "The Lovers". As expected. I nod and hover my hands over the pack to pick another. It shows a turbulent sky and five men pitching against each other. "The Five of Wands. Instability, conflicts, squabbling," I almost whisper. With a sharp flick, I pluck out the third card. There's a battleground with defeat and theft. "The Five of Swords. Deceit and dishonest dealings." I keep my voice neutral.

He gives an awkward laugh. "Aren't you supposed to tell me that I'll be meeting a tall, dark handsome stranger?"

I let the silence hang. "Your secret has been revealed to me," I stare deep into his eyes. His forehead throbs. "You've gone to great lengths to cover your tracks. But it's not enough. It's never enough."

I turn over his palm. It's sweating. "Cheating." His eyes narrow. "The thrill of the chase."

He pulls away. "Hey come on, you don't expect me to believe all this stuff do you?"

I shuffle the pack again and pull out The Tower. He looks at the body catapulted from a collapsing building, amongst rubble and lightning streaks. "Whatever lies ahead isn't fixed; you can take steps to change your fate. The Tower heralds a break up, the foundations of your life crumbling in on itself and crashing to the ground."

He frowns. His movements are impatient, so I rush to block the curtain. "The future position is mutable, it can be changed. I will be seeing your wife next, showing her predictions. I assume that you will be paying for both of you."

He tugs his wallet out of his back pocket and flings two twenty-pound notes on the table. I stand still and silent. I can see that there are a further couple of notes inside. He pulls one more out and disdainfully adds it to the pile.

"Men can pay a very high price for their indiscretions." Once the final note is thrown down, I step aside.

Often the wife has her own story: the tapping nails, fingers curling through her hair or scraping a pendant along a chain. The shadows and incense weave their magic.

His wife is pale. I notice that the smell in the room is too pungent. As swift as bats' wings, I reach out to extinguish the candle and open a window to fill the room with a slight, ruffling breeze. Her relief is palpable. I know

118

what I will find when I turn the cards. Her hands are clasped. I search her face as I reveal the Empress in her golden femininity with the One of Wands blazing like a flame. "I see a pregnancy." She looks up.

"A secret," I whisper, "in a small community, where people love to gossip." Her shudder isn't lost on me. "You will have a quiet weekend away with your husband, somewhere coastal and tell him the exciting news two weeks later."

She pays me fifty pounds without any prompting.

It's so important to read the signs. Anticipation is key. Often, I can get away with just reading three cards. I play the people, but faster is safer.

As dusk settles into darkness there's a pause, then I feel the tremor of the steps moving. Black boots are swallowed in a long dark woollen coat, like a shroud. A taut woman's face emerges. I have a stab of recognition, raw and stinging.

I draw backwards at the shimmering heat of her smouldering resentment. The tightness of the space is suffocating. A life can begin with a moment like this, or end.

Still, we must perform the ritual. Everything depends upon the turn of the cards. I can lie, but the Tarot cannot.

We take our positions, neither of us stirring. Repelling magnetic forces. The set of her jaw shows nights of teeth grinding.

The candle's scent is sickly sweet, but I feel pinned to the spot, unable to open a window. I reveal the cards in the present position: the Hanging Man and the Hermit, one prostrate and suspended, swinging from a chain, the other a stooped dark, solitary figure. "You are alone, introspective. And waiting." I don't need to look up because we both know that it's true.

She presents only a film of silence; we are caught in a duel without any parrying.

I want to rush the reading, but I lay out the deck with care to show the past. The waning wick elongates the shadowy lines in the fading light. "The Moon reveals illusory situations, deception and anxiety." My voice sounds different.

I stare straight into her ice-grey eyes; she doesn't flinch. Does she see the dark pools of loss, fear and guilt clogging mine?

The cards have taken control as I turn up the Nine and Ten of Swords, their sharp blades puncturing the flesh of a prone body. The breath is sucked out of me. "You have been suffering from disappointment, despair and distress." She exhales, almost extinguishing the candle.

A shot of pain bursts through me as I see his laughing eyes. I blink them away.

The clock is sounding slow and rhythmic against the racing of my pulse. I fight the urge to smash the glass, grab both hands and to crush them in my fist.

I rise; she stands too, with no intention of leaving.

So, we must continue until the end. "The card in the future position isn't fixed. You can take steps to change the outcome," I murmur, melting.

We are only one card away now from the end of the reading, but there's no relief to be found as I look into her stony eyes.

The air is still. Stifling. I rub my hand to steady it as I prepare to turn over the last card. It has a shadowy banner that billows across the top, like smoke from a pyre. The blackened skull is caught in its final grimace. Death.

Everyone has secrets. Not everyone likes to have them exposed.

Like a Lamb…

"He was oppressed, and he was afflicted, yet he opened not his mouth: he is brought as a lamb to the slaughter, and as a sheep before her shearers is dumb, so he openeth not his mouth."

Isiah 53.7

"Take care Maria!" My mother's voice echoed down the road. Not that I was really listening. *What does it even mean?* I wondered as I lurched towards a seat at the back of a bus and fell into it. *Do the drivers get extra points for the number of passengers they topple over?*

There wasn't much for me to do on the number 333 as it rattled through pools of light, before clattering around dark corners, so I snatched up a newspaper that was draped across the back seat. I flicked through the pages filled with the same old stories, using the same words: countries fighting, continents uniting, power struggles between nations, agreements shattered, allegiances broken. And the same for the people in the paper.

I thumbed through to the horoscopes. At the top of the page it said, "Follow your stars". So I did.

Then I realised that there are lots of stars, a sky full, so how do I know which one to follow?

The first three comets I chased burned themselves out rather quickly, but I gained greater wisdom about men, particularly the spiritual, venerable and estimable.

Even now, I can't smell the scent of myrrh without thinking about a director called Melchior. At first I was impressed by his gravitas, his neatly pressed charcoal suit and the gleaming black limo that he drove around in. Turned out that he was a funeral director and the gloomy face was his normal expression.

Now I don't know if you've ever become besotted by a priest, but let me tell you, it's fairly pointless. For one thing, Father Balthasar never noticed me as he had his eyes raised to heaven and for another it got quite chilly hanging around old churches whilst he wafted his frankincense about. Anyway, I learned my scriptures well.

The next seemed quite hopeful at first, an investment banker. Even I knew that I had gone from one extreme to another. Gaspar showered me with trinkets, (that he sent his secretary out to buy,) but not his time. Even I could only take so much jewellery, so in the end I pawned the gold and went travelling.

Whilst hitching a ride on a donkey cart I met Joe, a carpenter and a cabinet maker. *That's useful,* I thought, *a man who is good with his hands.*

We muddled along okay, although he used to sit bolt upright at night, disturbed by vivid dreams.

Then we had The Conversation. It seemed that we both had things on our mind. He shuffled in his seat in that shifty way that men sometimes do. Turned out that he had got behind on his tax returns and so he would have to travel to Jerusalem to sort it out, at the busiest time of year too.

Then it was my turn, so I told him that two of us would be joining him, as I was expecting a baby. He didn't exactly jump on his chair with joy, but that was probably just as well, as it was one that he'd made himself.

It was a somewhat bumpy journey in the donkey cart, so you can imagine my consternation when we finally arrived and he admitted that he hadn't booked ahead. The streets were thronging with people, so of course there was no accommodation left, not even an Airbnb.

So there I was, about to give birth in a busy town, engaged to an impoverished furniture restorer and staying in a manky outbuilding without so much as a stick of furniture.

No sooner had we settled in, than my contractions started. As if that wasn't bad enough, we were both shaken by a great flash of blinding light, the walls shook and rubble flew against the building.

"That's it!" I yelled above the noise. "As soon as this baby's born we're outta here!" We're not waiting around for a bomb to fall on us. Herod's men have killed enough babies and children already!"

Joe nodded and softly added, "We'll make our way to Egypt."

With all the chaos going on around us, I didn't want to risk going to the hospital. There could not have been a worse time to give birth.

Luckily my baby was born very quickly, but oh my word, I don't want to go through that again in a hurry! Even the shepherds in the neighbouring field came scurrying down to check that I was okay, like I needed an audience. Anyway, they told me that they knew how to help, having birthed numerous sheep in the fields, so I guess for them it was just one more lamb.

I sent WhatsApp photos of my beautiful baby boy to my family, friends, exes and all those people who had forgotten about me, before sleeping, utterly exhausted.

The following morning Joe leapt up to a banging on the door. There were three Next Day Signed For deliveries. Luckily he got there before they tried to shove a "We tried to deliver" card through the letter box.

My baby boy blinked open his eyes as we unwrapped the three gifts in front of him: gold from Gaspar, Frankincense from Balthasar and myrrh from Melchior.

I leant over and tucked the blankets around him, protecting his soft skin. His little mouth puckered. I stroked his rounded cheek and allowed his tiny hand to clasp my finger. He lit up my world. As I pulled him close to me I felt overwhelmed by the urge to save him from evil, danger or harm. My son, my love, my life.

_____

Published in *Nativity*, December 2018, Bridge House.

A Cracker for One

Even before the phone call Etisha felt spiky, as though electrical currents were jarring through her. The Sellotape crackled as she pulled out a strip whilst holding a flap of paper under her thumb. *Christmas, why doesn't someone cancel it?*

Groaning she fumbled for the buzzing phone in her jeans pocket, as the tape stuck together in loops. Charlie the spaniel darted towards it hopefully as she flung it across the floor.

"Not again John! You said you'd be home tonight. It's Christmas Eve for heaven's sake!"

"Not now Etisha. Look this is important."

"Yes, yes, your job serves the national interests, security, blah blah."

"Etisha listen to me, please. This is important. Can you go into the garage a moment?"

"Don't tell me you've bought me a new car for Christmas."

"Seriously E, you need to listen. We don't have much time."

Etisha flicked on the fluorescent strip light and shivered as she stepped onto the cold concrete floor. "About Christmas… What I said. I didn't mean it, well, not all of it anyway."

"I know. Look Etisha, we can't talk about any of this now. Have you found the stuff I've put in the garage? It's all under the black tarpaulin, next to your empty boxes for the decorations."

"Uh huh," she replied, resting the phone against her shoulder and peeling back the black sheet. "That's a strange present: a bag full of medical supplies. Now why would I be needing antibiotics? This is very odd John. When will you be home to explain?"

"That's the reason why I'm calling, and you must leave home too. Go now. But first load up the car whilst we're talking. Take the black hybrid 4 x 4 which I've filled with petrol."

"Why?"

"It will get you to Devon, cross country if necessary, without you needing to stop at a garage."

"No, why leave home, and why Devon?"

"Look Etisha, we're anticipating a cyber-attack, on a scale we haven't seen before. We thought we had the technical capability to stop it, we're still trying, but…"

"What, like bombs exploding or banks hacked into? A big bang? The world ending like it began?"

"No," he sighed, "electricity."

She sat on a box. "You mean some sort of power cut?"

Sensing her lack of motion he urged, "Keep packing the car as we speak. These are the bare essentials to get you through the next few days."

"Will they have power in Devon?"

"Unlikely. Supplies have already gone down through all of Scotland. Intelligence thinks London will be next, then the home counties. This outage is probably going to be an electrical failure on a national scale, with unimaginable consequences."

"My sister is in Newcastle."

"I've sent her a text; it's all I had time for. I told her to head towards the national parks."

Etisha groaned as she hauled a five gallon container towards the car. "Water? Are you sure?"

"Take everything there." An edge had crept into his voice. "The tap water supply might become contaminated." More gently, "Prepare yourself for people panicking. Looting will begin in shops after just a day, but will soon extend to cars and homes. The stores will shut down, but

126

their supplies won't last for more than three days anyway. Avoid the towns."

"A gun?" she squealed.

"Take it. It's better to be where the food is grown or can be hunted. Make sure you get beyond Hinkley Point, the nuclear power point in Somerset."

"What?"

"Head for Dartmoor. Once the nuclear back-up generators run out of fuel their rods will over heat, causing explosions and fire. In any case they will be the first points to be attacked once our military defences are compromised."

She dragged tins and packets of dried food across to the car and heaved them into the back, watching as it dipped downwards.

"The hospitals?"

"Most hospitals will be OK with their emergency generators for a while, as long as they can keep a subsistence staff in place."

She flung the dog bowls and bags of kibble into the boot.

"Hurry Etisha! You should be leaving now!"

"Clothes?" she commented, picking up khaki waterproofs with fleece linings. "Not quite what I would have chosen. An extra can of petrol. You've certainly thought of everything."

His voice sounded echoey and far away. "Whatever you do, don't take the motorways. Roads will quickly become gridlocked once there's a mass evacuation of the towns. Trapped people become panicked people, particularly when they find themselves without food, drink or blankets."

She wrapped the candles in glass holders along with the matches and lighter into the woollen blankets and piled these on top. In between the seats she wedged the battery powered radio, alongside some spare flashlights, a pan, implements and a stove. As an afterthought she scooped up the cover thrown over the decorations' boxes and draped this over everything.

"Also on your route, avoid main roads with traffic lights. They'll stop working soon. Country lanes are best, whenever possible. Put the map and flashlight on the seat next to you, as well as Charlie. Mobile phones and Sat Navs will be useless."

She clicked Charlie's harness on. "So when can you join me?"

His voice seemed to fade, a door shut and she heard footsteps. "Where are you?"

"No, Etisha, I'm sorry, I can't. Don't wait. Go now. I…" The line went dead.

Infuriated Etisha re-dialled. "This can't be happening. Tell me it's not happening!" she yelled into the answer phone.

Charlie whined and looked towards the car with a hopeful thud of his tail.

She took a last look at the Christmas tree laced with tinsel, then like a sleepwalker, she closed the door on her past life. The string of lights around the house waved in the breeze.

They sped past lit up houses, inflatable snowmen and urgently flashing lights. On the slip road she remembered that she had forgotten her handbag which held her cards and money. *How could she have been so stupid?* She accelerated into the lane before realising two things: The ATMs would stop working, so what use would money be? She'd ignored John's advice and without thinking she had joined the motorway.

Above her she saw circling arcs of planes that could not land into Heathrow. Air traffic control would stop. Airports could not operate. She tried not to be distracted by the chaos and confusion in the air above her.

At first the miles flashed past, as the M4 merged into the M5, the traffic thickening, but moving. The radio played *'Tis the season to be jolly!* She switched the dial, trying to avoid the interference. She needed the news.

Ahead she saw the red lights stacking up, car upon car. Her speed faltered, slowly edging forward, finally stationary. She fumbled with the radio again, "…gridlocked traffic across the arterial motorways." Crackles burst in. "Reports of a power cut due to a suspected power surge, causing panic buying in supermarkets." It broke off and the cars nudged forward slightly. *Coming home for Christmas* played. *John, he even thought to buy tissues.*

She jolted as a news flash interrupted the music. "Accounts have just come in that the Thames barrier hasn't closed properly, causing widespread flooding in parts of London and surrounding areas. We don't know yet the scale of the damage, or if there are any casualties."

John, take care, wherever you are.

As the wait lengthened, stretching into an hour without movement, Etisha felt her palms become clammy. *How could she have made such a foolish mistake?*

She managed to pick up another news station and against the hissing interference she could just discern, "There are reports that customers have become trapped in some stores as the electronic doors have stopped opening. The Government urges everyone to remain calm, but has advised that it is better to remain indoors and to avoid travelling. They have warned against using any lifts, but to take the stairs if possible."

People started to step out of their cars to stretch their legs. First one man sauntered up and down beside the vehicles, then he was joined by others. She was glad that she had covered up her provisions and that her car had blackened windows. Etisha slammed the button to lock the doors and sunk into her seat.

Horns hooted, first in impatient humour, then with increasing agitation. She would have liked to give Charlie a bit of a walk, but she couldn't risk abandoning her car.

Etisha drummed her feet on the floor, looking around, fiddling with the edges of the covers. Plumes of yellow smoke were visible in the distance, coming from a near-by town.

Still she kept checking her phone for a missed call from her sister, a message from John. Anything. In the back she found a dog treat for Charlie and rummaged through some of the boxes. One toothbrush. He had never intended to join her.

She lay her head back against the seat rest, dozing slightly and losing track of time. Suddenly a bang on the window brought her upright. Charlie growled as a man stood by the door. She looked away. She would not open it. She played with the radio knobs once again. Silence.

Only then did she realise that the railway running alongside was motionless. *Of course, no trains.*

Etisha held her breath as one by one the motorway signs were extinguished. Distant towns which were jewelled with golden glowing lights became black chasms.

So it's happening, it's really happening.

Leaning across the seat, Etisha shone the torch on her outstretched map, planning her route with a shaky finger. She started the ignition. She couldn't wait. Taking a deep breath, she accelerated on to the hard shoulder. Immediately other vehicles followed in her wake. At the roundabout she went straight across, aware of the queues of traffic stacking up to join the motorway.

She cut a sharp left at some darkened traffic lights,

bolting through and narrowly missing a squealing van. Taking a deep breath, she counted three more A roads before she could head cross country.

Her thudding heart was only accompanied by the soft purr of her engine. She passed houses that were as black as tombs, with just the occasional flickering candle.

Closer to Dartmoor the traffic crawled once more. Even the adjoining roads looked gridlocked. Etisha braced herself and cut across a farmer's field. The car mounted the ridge with a bump, she leapt out to swing open the gate and revved it forward with the engine screeching. Several times it skidded in the squelching mud, but she swerved ahead, her instinct warning her to find seclusion.

It was then that she realised that she was lost, helplessly lost. She fingered in the side compartment and put a mint in her mouth. With only her headlights and a crescent moon to guide her, charcoal silhouettes of trees seemed to leap out at her as she bumped along. Feeling lightheaded she stopped. "Time for a walk Charlie," she whispered into the merging blackness.

Even Charlie was quiet as they clambered out. "All we can do is put one foot in front of the other and fumble along," she said, gently fondling his ears and releasing his harness. She thought about those virtual games where the character had to progress in darkness through various levels of difficulty, only this was the raw, real world.

The sharp scythe of the moon scarcely cut into the pitch blackness. Even the beam of light from her torch seemed to only accentuate the surrounding walls of darkness.

The air did not move, as though waiting. It was strange to be out in such stillness. Such absolute silence.

They trudged across a ridged field before Etisha began to question the wisdom of leaving the car. As she flashed the arc of light onto misshapen tree stumps, she murmured to Charlie trotting beside her, "We have to try to gain some sense of this area." He looked up with his bright, trusting brown eyes.

The slam of a door alerted them to wisps of smoke coming from a distant chimney. A hedge loomed ahead, obscuring a stone cottage. For a moment she paused, blinking back memories of a cosy armchair, mulled wine and television.

She switched off the torch. Charlie growled. "Hello!" she called. Nothing. "Is anyone there?" No response.

An instinct made Etisha look towards the shed door, where she saw the glint of a long barrel gleaming in the moonlight.

Charlie barked. She lowered herself. Two shots burst through the night, rupturing the silence.

Charlie, where was he? Had he bolted? How would he find her in this thick, impenetrable darkness? What if he had been shot? All she could do was run, unaware of the direction, but away from the cottage, stumbling over mounds of earth, slipping, sliding. Her breath came out in plumes. "Charlie," she whispered, "Charlie, where are you?"

She had to risk the flashlight so that he could see her. Louder now, an edge of desperation seeping into her voice, "Charlie! Charlie, here boy! Treats!"

Nothing. She listened for the clink of his collar, her eyes focused to try to see his flapping ears or his black nose sniffing the ground.

Etisha spun around, throwing the light in a circle around her. *Had he been spooked? Or was he chasing foxes?*

Which direction had she come from? Which way must she go?

"Charlie!" she cried. "Charlie, come now! I don't even know how to find the car!"

A straggly bush emerged in front of her, but she was uncertain whether it was the same one or different, they all looked the identical in the darkness. She edged around it, heading towards some shadowy trees.

Suddenly a green light lit up on her phone. Etisha stared at it. A message. She fumbled to look at it. "Take care, wherever you are. Don't go back. John x." Sent seven hours ago. She looked up through the lattice work of branches at the cold, distant stars and blinked.

The phone blackened and died.

As she stumbled forward she saw the glinting edges of her car. There, sitting by the bonnet and waiting patiently for her return was Charlie.

Etisha caved forward, wrapping her arms around him and nuzzling his soft fur. Engulfed in a rush of light headed relief which bordered on exhilaration, she held her dog. They were alone. Frightened. Free.

She flung the phone in a puddle. It was no use to her now. Tomorrow she would find somewhere more suitable to hide her car, somewhere more secluded.

Tomorrow she realised would be Christmas Day. But Christmas had been cancelled.

Etisha pulled out the blanket covering the boot of her car. Something fluttered to the ground. "Tonight Charlie, we will be safe enough sleeping here," she said as she pulled on the fleece lined top and trousers. She slammed the boot shut with a bundle of blankets in her arms.

Etisha peered at the ground to see what had fallen. A single golden cracker lay slumped in the mud.

Published in the *CaféLit Magazine* 22nd December 2020.

Snowdrop

"If you make friends with yourself you will never be alone."

Maxwell Maltz

"The caged bird sings with a fearful trill, of things unknown, but longed for still, and his tune is heard on the distant hill, for the caged bird sings of freedom."

Maya Angelou

Fluttering flakes swirled in a dance, celebrating their uniqueness. Silently, stealthily they settled, merging and losing their identity in one solid mass of snow.

At first the heavy door to the wooden chalet seemed wedged shut. Sylvie scraped back some more of the burgeoning, compacted snow from the step and wrenched it open, just a slither, but enough to slide through.

A chill permeated the room as she swept the ash from the grate. All around her she could see signs of the last visit, the red wine circles bled onto the oak coffee table, dishevelled cushions sloping off the sofa and the runched up crimson rug.

She coaxed a flame to shimmer into life and sat back on her haunches as it flickered against the wall. It was not so very long ago; it was another person, a different life time. Only shades from the past danced in the shadowy fireplace.

Sunlight filtered through the slats in the green shutters, enticing her awake. They creaked open with a languorous stretch, allowing the dazzling brightness to burst into the room.

Iridescent, sparkling drops twirled outside the window, gracefully gliding to the ground.

She longed to rush outside, crunching her boots in the crispy snow, indenting pools of her own footprints.

These are my daisy chain days, she sighed, savouring this moment of happiness. Yesterday on the sleigh they felt exhilarated and alive, tumbling, twisting, hurtling down the mountain, with their scarves thrown out behind them.

Flocculent snow flew into their hair, flowed onto their tongues, feathery, fleecy and flimsy as confetti. Their cries swirled into the billowing veil.

With flushed cheeks they had built up the fire, its rosy glow suffusing the room with warmth. Sylvie had placed a flickering cinnamon candle on the coffee table and stood back to watch the burnished walnut basking in the honey glow.

She watched the soporific movement of his breath as he lay cocooned inside the soft, downy duvet. Sylvie snuggled up to the warm, white mound.

Flurries of flakes fluttered past, drifting and floating into a lacy lattice curtain which covered the window.

Her eye lids fluttered shut as she drifted back into dreams, her world obscured beneath the white chill.

Fleeting flakes seemed to dwindle into the opaque clouds.

He had not been answering her emails or returning her calls. Just one terse answer-phone message about work commitments.

Finally she broke through and the words tumbled out of her, falling into the vacuum of his pristine white sitting room.

Her legs were spread out on the sofa; lingerie was flung out from the carrier bag and provocatively sprawled across the coffee table.

"Yep," his voice sounded muffled, as though he was shovelling a load of crisps into his mouth.

Sylvie tried to keep her voice light and airy. In the background she could hear a football commentary. "How was your day?"

"Yeah… good." The commentary appeared to have been turned up a little, or else he had moved closer to the television.

"So what have you been doing?"

"Oh… this and that, you know."

Not really she thought, *or I would not be asking.*

"Me too. Just arrived at the chalet. It's not the same without you."

"Uh huh." She could hear cheering in the background.

"Before leaving I thought I'd check up on my dad to make sure that he would be all right for the next few days."

"Uh huh."

"He'd set fire to the microwave again."

"Uh huh."

"This time he put his socks into the oven to try to dry them."

"Oh."

"Still, at least he remembered to keep the door shut this time, and the fire brigade know the short cut to his house now."

"Mmmm."

"It's such a shame that you couldn't join me. It has been a year since we've been to the chalet together. I know you've taken some business clients here, but I mean just the two of us, to relax properly." She tried to keep the whine out of her voice.

"Work," he sighed. "You know I can't afford to take the time off."

"Perhaps I should have postponed flying to the chalet?" She paused. "Stayed a bit longer to keep you company?"

Bleary flakes smothered the window and slid slowly downwards.

136

"Oh no!" he groaned, in unison with the crowd on the television. "No, no, it's fine, you enjoy it," his voice was fast, dismissive.

It was hard to hide the edge of disappointment, to still sound bright, without recrimination, without nagging. "I had been so looking forward to our time alone together," she searched for the usual trigger words, "stockings, steak."

"Yes," he responded, "all good."

It felt like an own goal.

"Tricky," she replied, "with a few hundred miles between us."

"Poor reception," he grunted. "I can't hear you properly."

"Yes," she agreed, "I seem to be losing you."

Sylvie shivered, feeling the cold wind increase as it rattled the windows and slunk beneath the door. Spinning swirls of snow were whipped up, whirled and flung against the pane.

Fleeting flakes stealthily slunk around the chalet, obliterating the landscape.

She stepped downstairs, surrounded by the resounding silence. The heavy air fell away from her.

Logs collapsed back into the grate, spitting sparks. It felt as though the breath had been punched from inside her, leaving an aching hollowness.

Flames flew up the chimney, casting shadows, whispering secrets. Hidden, yet known.

The mantelpiece mirror threw back the map of her face, refracted in the amber light; each line tracing a new road, the difficult terrain she had crossed, her journey.

Outside the platinum clouds held back the early morning sun rays. Cushions of snow squashed beneath her boots, spongy and squelching.

Slumped backed mountains surrounded her, slumbering beneath their snowy folds. Pine trees drooped, laden and ready to drop their heavy load.

Sylvie smiled, the wrinkles etched like stars under her eyes. Shivering in the sharp wind stood a small, solitary snowdrop. A mound of snow had parted around the flower, as it waited for the first glimmer of sunlight to break through from behind the mountains.

Little by little, small verdant blotches will seep their way through the snow; tiny islands that will spread and merge.

Soon the mountains would be flooded with a profusion of wild flowers, in rivers of crimson, amber and violet. Tomorrow.

Today she had the nodding snowdrop, alone and lovely. It had broken through the crystalline snow on its slender green stem, hanging its modest white head.

––––––––––––

Published in *Snowflakes*, November 2015, Bridge House.

Wake Up and Smell the Roses

"Perfume is the art that makes memory speak."
Francis Kukdjian

"Perfume heralds a woman's arrival and prolongs her departure."
Coco Chanel

Some people believe that when strong emotions are involved in an unresolved situation, it can play out forever... It cannot be stopped; a perpetual wheel of motion, like the planets orbiting the Sun or the Earth turning.

Ruth led Tom by the hand across the velvety lawn of Willow Manor, like a dog on a lead. He followed, pausing only to crumble some lavender stalks between his fingers, or to inspect the herbs by the box hedges.

In his own scent garden, he had several varieties of lavender, as well as sweet smelling honeysuckle and deep crimson roses. It was amongst the flowers that he found peace, where he could allow his mind to drift off in clouds of pollen. So, it was correct that he should propose to Ruth there; he had done the right thing. Not that it had been unexpected; she had already chosen her ring.

Tom allowed her voice to dip in and out, like the drone of a bee, requiring only the occasional nod of his head. The late afternoon sun's rays slanted across the grass, casting elongated oval, coniferous shadows.

Ruth's voice rose a pitch, conveying her excitement as her step sprung off the lawn, "It's so lucky that Lady Blade is one of your best customers. To think that the manor house will only open up four times a year and she has allowed us to have one of these occasions for our wedding!"

Lady Blade's perfume, Tom recalled, had aspidistra notes, with a deep woody base. Each of his scents was carefully blended, perfect for its recipient and then placed in unique glass bottles. Lady Blade's was in a water carrier shape with a gold button lid.

Tom believed that scent should be as unique as a fingerprint, identifying a person the moment that they entered a room. The perfume would become part of their aura, blending into the atmosphere.

There was one perfume though, that stood alone on the sill, unclaimed. It was Tom's special scent, a soft blend of jasmine, rose and honeysuckle, with just a hint of cherry blossom. This was poured into a curved glass bottle, which was sprinkled with tiny sparkling silver stars. He kept it in a crimson velvet box, unclaimed, almost forgotten.

Then it happened, but not as Tom had anticipated.

He was alone in the shop, staring at the swelling purple sky, blotched with grey clouds, until these became blotted out into a scowling blackened mass. Tom wiped his hand across his brow as he tried to mix together different aromas for Ruth's wedding perfume, but the disparate smells kept jarring and no matter how he varied the quantities, they would not blend. A rumble of thunder announced the release of rain drops the size of pebbles, drumming a persistent knock against the door and windows. Tom checked that the shuddering catchments were closed, his pulse quickening with a sense of anticipation.

The oak eaves above him moaned and groaned, like the creaking timber masts of a floundering ship. The wind whipped up the brass front door knocker, with a frenetic, urgent pulse of movement.

After a few resounding metallic slaps, Tom peered more closely, as a shadowy figure seemed to be standing outside. He rushed to release the catch and the door burst open, flung by the wind against the inside wall. No-one was standing there. He peered around the outside edge of the white-washed building, into the swirling rain. Nothing.

He returned to his counter, oddly reluctant to withdraw upstairs. The door rattled as though it was being shaken off its hinges.

With the sleeve of his jacket, he wiped a circle in the misted-up window. The rain slid down the panes, illuminated by the amber glow of the outside lamps. At first, he saw only a reflection of his white face and dark eyes staring back in the cleared circle of the smudged window.

Then he saw them. The eyes. Large gleaming hazel eyes stared straight back at him.

Her skin was pale, her hair streaming with rivulets of water rushing down. He couldn't tear his gaze away, as he became drawn deeper and deeper into those dark eyes. His whole being seemed to become swallowed up in an overwhelming sense of misery, which seemed to hollow out his insides, leaving an aching emptiness.

Tom knew then that the perfume was hers; she had come to claim it. He felt along the sill for the velvet box and flung the door open into the wild, blustery night.

She was gone.

Still he ran, seeking, searching, unable to cease. Flickers of lightning forked the sky, but did not provide enough light through the impenetrable rain. He could not stop.

Only when a plaintive voice called his name did he halt, for the first time noticing that his clothes had become weighted down with water and his hair was plastered against his head. Under an umbrella, Ruth ran over to him. Her eyes narrowed as she took in his sopping clothes.

"Tom? I thought it must be you. What on earth are you doing? Whatever's the matter? What has happened to you?"

He found himself unable to answer; the pervasive sense of sorrow seemed to seep into his bones.

Tom looked at his hands which were now empty; he was no longer clutching the perfume bottle.

Tutting, Ruth led him back to his shop, as he glanced behind him, wondering where he had dropped the bottle. She wrapped him in a large woollen blanket and he allowed her ministrations to stop his chattering teeth. In front of the crackling fire, the blood flowed once more through his veins and he shook his head at his strange fancy. The events disappeared like the wispy smoke up the chimney.

A voice clattered into his thoughts, disturbing his reverie.

"Tom! Are you coming?" He raised his head to see Ruth standing with her hands on her hips, feet planted squarely on the lawn, a gesture he was sure he would see a great deal of in the future. Recovering, he pointed to a flowerbed full of Michaelmas Daisies and asked, "Have you decided which flowers you will have in your wedding bouquet yet?"

Ruth shook her head, her brow furrowed. "Tom, do come on, we'll be late! It wouldn't do to keep Lady Blade's housekeeper waiting!"

Her face was sharp with impatience. He lengthened his strides, stepping over the slatted, shadowy grounds and as he did so, he experienced a heightened sense of expectation, as though he was finally arriving at a long-awaited destination.

The sandstone walls of Willow Manor glowed in the tawny sunset as they stepped through the arched doorway and tapped briskly along a polished wooden floor. Eleanor Brown smiled with efficient courtesy as she gestured towards a chair with golden damask covers, backed by flouncing gilt scrolls. "Do take a seat."

Tom perched on the edge whilst Ruth ran an appraising eye over the honeycombed ceiling, from which sparkling chandeliers drooped. Mottled marble pillars in each corner of the room flanked the tapestried walls.

Eleanor opened her arms wide, with evident pride. "This is the drawing room for drinks. I will take you to the main reception room in a moment. Perhaps you would like to have a copy of the menu from the catering company?" she suggested as she placed it into Ruth's lap.

Ruth flipped through the pages as Tom's eyes darted around. Apple tree wood was crackling in the grate, emitting a sweet scent as it flung up purple green sparks.

"Goodness, in a place like this, you could almost believe in ghosts," laughed Ruth as she glanced upwards. Eleanor's enigmatic smile was reflected in the sparkling mirrors, which gleamed on each wall, reflecting the willows outside in the deepening dusk. In turn, the windows shone back the amber glow of the lamps, strategically placed upon skirted tables.

Out of the corner of his eye, Tom caught something moving. At first, he was too disorientated to know whether it was inside or outside the room. He sat up. A figure flickered past the window, and then halted. For a moment their eyes locked through the pane, before she slipped away.

He pointed. "Who's that? Is she real?"

"Very much so," replied Eleanor. "That's Alicia, Lady Blade's daughter, on a rare visit. She spends most of her time in Switzerland."

Next to him, Tom sensed Ruth giving him a side-long glance as he sunk back into the chair.

Into the silence Eleanor said, "All great houses have their stories. I expect you've heard the legend of Willow Manor?"

Tom looked doubtful, while Ruth shook her head.

"Well, the last sighting goes back fifty years ago, or more now, so in neither of your life times. It caused quite a stir in the village, although people seldom speak of it now."

"Sighting?" queried Ruth, as she scanned the menu.

Eleanor nodded. "It all began uneventfully enough. A village craftsman, a carpenter, was betrothed to the local seamstress, Mary, who worked at Willow Manor. Arrangements were being made for their nuptials, when the lady of the manor took them under her wing and offered a small celebration in the grounds of the great house. Naturally, they were delighted, but it was during the preparations that Tim, the carpenter met the daughter, Alice. At first neither spoke, but as Tim was making a stage for a barn dance in the cattle shed near the stables, they kept seeing each other.

"Although they didn't intend to fall in love, they did and they couldn't help but show it. Once the Blade family found out, there was outrage, they were forbidden to see each other and the wedding was called off."

Ruth looked up, intrigued.

"They planned to elope during the dark of the moon, but probably weren't discreet enough, as their plans may have been overheard. A servant later said that she saw Alice disappearing into the dark night, with her cloak flying out behind her, carrying just a small travelling bag. Tim waited and waited, his agitation no doubt increasing with each hour that crept by.

"She never arrived.

"The following morning Alice was found drowned in the mill pond, although her bag had been left in a field nearby. They never discovered the cause; whether the noble family had tried unsuccessfully to make her return and killed her in a rage, or perhaps Alice had a jealous admirer?

In the stormy weather Alice might have misplaced her footing in the dark, or even the carpenter's fiancée, Mary might have harmed her in a rage. All we know is that Tim was never the same again."

Tom shook his head.

"That should have been where the story ended," continued Eleanor, "but over the last century there have been a few reported sightings of Alice, especially on the anniversary of her death, on blustery, rainy nights, similar to the one she perished in.

"Mary, the seamstress, forgave Tim and they married in the village church. You can see the entry on the Parish records. Not that it seemed to bring him much happiness.

"Afterwards Tim seemed to waste away, hollows sunk under his eyes, his cheeks became gaunt and his face looked cadaverous, so in the end he became a morose shadow of himself."

A stillness settled in the room, with just the rhythmic tick of the clock.

Ruth broke in, "I guess most of these old houses have some history."

"Yes," agreed Eleanor, "you can see portraits of the ancestors lined up along the grand staircase. The strange thing is that the painting of Alice looks so like Alicia, it's uncanny."

"Not really," said Ruth. "After all, they are related."

"Can I take a look?" asked Tom as he rose to his feet. Ruth's back stiffened.

"Well yes, of course, whilst I run through the menus with Ruth," she said pointing towards the main entrance.

With a hammering heart, Tom flung himself out of the room. The oak staircase curved in front of him, but already he could see Alice's portrait poised mid-way, her raised chin seeming to challenge him.

As he climbed upwards the air smelt sweet, with notes of jasmine, cherry-blossom, rose and honeysuckle suspended in the air. The higher he climbed, the stronger the scent, the harder his heart drummed.

The hazel eyes drew him level, the angry green sparks flashing a silent fury. His breathing slowed. Transfixed, he stood, drawn into a communion of recognition. The cloud of perfume seemed to cloy his senses.

What happened next, he would never really know.

Perhaps he stood too close to the painting, or accidentally knocked it? He was only aware of the portrait seeming to lift off the wall and falling towards him. He wasn't even sure whether he put his arm out to catch it, or to protect himself. The side of the frame landed with a crashing thump at his feet whilst the portrait drummed against the floor, reverberating as it crashed from side to side.

It all seemed to happen in slow motion, as his feet lost their balance and he fell sideways, tumbling down the staircase. His head made impact with the floor at the same moment that the portrait dropped face downwards. Neither moved.

The stench of antiseptic was over-powering, but when Tom tried to push away from it, the tightly bound hospital sheets held him in place. He could not find the strength to resist.

A fuzzy face loomed over him. "That was quite a scare." His eyelids flickered open to see Ruth adjusting the blanket. "Honestly, for a moment I thought that I'd lost you."

He touched the bandages with tentative fingers.

"It's okay," she smiled, "just a broken wrist with fractured forearm which you held out to protect yourself, and some concussion. It could have been much worse. How are you feeling now?"

Tom gave a nauseous shake of the head. "It's all a bit of a blur. I remember my body caving in on itself and falling towards the floor. I felt dizzy with everything spinning as I went bumping down the stairs, unable to stop or to catch myself."

"None of us knew what was happening. First, we heard a loud bang, which must have been that heavy portrait falling off the wall, followed by the thumping of you falling down the stairs.

"We all jumped out of our seats." Her eyes narrowed. "But Alicia was at the front entrance and so she reached you first. It looked like you were dead! She wouldn't stop screaming! In the end we had to call two ambulances, one for her to give some kind of sedative, and one for you.

"Lady Blade decided to send Alicia back to her special clinic in Switzerland. The incident wasn't good for her nervous condition and she was afraid that it might have set her back a bit. She had made arrangements to manage it, but they won't be necessary now."

He smelt a suffocating clinical, antiseptic smell and something else, something sweet, chloroform perhaps?

Ruth looked away from Tom to open a window. A draft ruffled some papers which were spread across his bed and he shuddered, in spite of the blankets.

"It was a nasty fall you had there and a shock like that isn't good for someone with your, well, artistic temperament, either."

Tom raised an eyebrow, but Ruth ploughed on, unnecessarily smoothing the sheet in front of her. "Anyway, I've been thinking and I've decided to cancel the booking with Lady Blade for our wedding venue."

Tom released a slow breath. He felt lighter.

"Under the circumstances, I am sure she will understand. I don't think a big wedding would be good for you – and your excitable nature, not to mention your injuries. I've spoken to the consultant and he thinks that you will be out of here in three or four days.

"So, I've booked us in at the local registry office, nothing fancy, all very low key, for a week's time. Then I will be able to look after you until you recover properly."

Tom looked into Ruth's slate eyes and saw endless grey skies stretched out before him, with neither sunshine nor storm.

There was something unsaid, out of reach and Tom struggled to grasp it. "Under the circumstances? You mean my accident?"

Ruth shuffled in her chair. "Well yes, that and Alicia's unfortunate accident."

Tom sat up, his eyes widening as he stared into her impassive face.

A gust of wind blew through the window and flung the documents up into Ruth's face like angry pigeons. She pushed them aside, her eyes as cold as steel. "I wasn't going to mention the incident until you were fully recovered, but I expect you will hear about it from a visitor. As I said, Alicia had a bit of an uncertain temperament. Last night she was found dead, drowned in the village mill pond."

She laid a firm hand on his arm, as tight as a manacle.

He sunk back, his head spinning, turning, swirling in a blurry whirl of half remembered moments.

Eyebeam

*"Why beholdest thou the mote that is in thy brother's
eye, but considerest not the beam that is in thine own
eye?"*

Matthew 7:3

Swirls of mist surrounded the lighthouse, entwining it in
chiffon ribbons. Strobing beams fought to burst through,
only to rebound and merge in the pervasive whiteness.

Ben reached for the off-grid recording equipment and
pressed the switch, feeling his chest tighten. When he had
been assigned to record the signs of spirit activity at
Stainmouth Lighthouse for the Chronicle's Halloween
issue he had laughed, actually laughed. Now as he watched
the spirals of fog coiling around the lighthouse and
cocooning it into its own watery white world, the stories
felt far less improbable.

He had to keep busy, to take a professional approach.
He pulled out a pen and notebook to begin compiling a list
of sightings. Most seemed to occur in the window room,
which seemed odd. Page after page were plucked from the
book and strewn across the table. He clambered up the
rickety honeycombed spiral staircase which wound around
like a coiled shell. He placed a camera looking straight
down, another looking up. Some were directed towards the
windows but most were turned towards the wooden space
dotted with dark mahogany furniture, like a stage set.

There were the sounds that he would need to pick up: a
bell clanging, footfalls, sobbing, moaning, scraping,
shrieking.

The air chilled around him, so he shook his arms into a
fleece. He could do with contacting a friend now to make
light of the situation. Shame about the lack of reception.

He remembered the banter in the office when Larry, the junior reporter had been sent to cover the Spirit in the Lighthouse story, but been too scared to stay the night. He became the butt of all their jokes. Ben didn't rate Larry, he seemed too spooked by his own shadow. It made him fair game, livened up their days. Ben smirked as he recalled Larry's face as he took a slurp of the only coffee Ben had ever made him, laced with chilli powder at the bottom.

He liked to amuse Maureen, such as the time he sent Larry off on an assignment to interview the vicar's talking cat. Maureen would reproach him for laughing at Larry, then snigger like a steam train.

Ben did feel a bit bad about stitching up Larry's promotion by altering some of his final copy. Of course, no-one could prove it was him; he'd covered his tracks too well. And Larry was too wet behind the ears to mentor the trainee reporters, they'd walk all over him. Really, he'd done him a favour.

He just had to get through a few hours. After all, what difference would one night make? The story could be huge, not just locally, but nationally. Hits on the website and ratings would be off the scale…

Ben checked the equipment again. Good that he'd thought to make it a local recording for a remote area.

The oozing fog seemed to sink over the lighthouse, seeping into the white walls and windows, so that it became hard to distinguish those from the swirling mist outside and the frothing sea. Even the beams of light were smothered in the blinding, shifting vapours, split into the haze and flung back.

Ben shuddered as he realised that the malevolent force might lie within these curved walls, not without. A clammy darkness dropped suddenly. An aura spun over the tower, the rest of the world was obscured.

Ben gritted his teeth. The secret was to stay awake. The strange happenings always occurred while the occupant slept. He sat upright on the stiff wooden chair, gazing into the blurry whiteness.

He maintained his vigil until 3 am. Softly his breathing slowed, keeping time with the pulse of light. Edges blurred, the hazy windows and walls melted, as he floated off in a shuddering, luminous bubble.

The next events seemed to happen without any kind of order. A door slammed. The light bulb swung like a metronome, hypnotically in time with the outside beams. A cracking of wood. The tinkling of glass. A pounding of heavy footsteps shaking the floor.

Then it happened: the fog warning bell. Insistently it reverberated around the room, clanging its echoing warning of danger.

Outside the waves battered the rocks. A shrill shriek. Banging. A pounding, hammering on the door. Demanding entry.

Ben's body lay splayed across the wooden floor. Sprawled around him were cracked chair legs, daggers of glass and a toppled table. The door vibrated from the pummelling fists. A weak yellow light filtered through the windows as the sea flailed outside.

His body felt sore and heavy. Still the thumping continued, in time with his heart bursting from his chest. He lay in a heap of destruction.

As though mesmerised, he lumbered to grab the handle, wrenched it open and blinked.

"I waited until 6.00, then I thought I'd better check on you. What the hell happened?" Larry peered around the door. "You okay?"

Ben nodded, gestured with his arm to come in and slumped on the floor.

Larry surveyed the scene and went over to check the equipment. His face froze as he scanned the recording.

"What's the matter?" asked Ben, alarmed. "Don't tell me that the vile spectre smashed that up too!"

"No," Larry's voice was scarcely audible. "It's all intact."

"What then? Oh no!" Ben sat up. "Don't tell me that none of it recorded! Don't say that I went through all of that for nothing!"

Larry stared into the viewfinder and replied softly, "No, it's clear."

"Look, if I can get through a night like that, surely I can see the footage. I've got the worst behind me."

Still Larry held the recording, his look intense.

"What's wrong?" Ben's voice faltered. "Do you think I can't take it or something?"

"I don't know," Larry mumbled. "I'll wait for you outside."

Ben gripped the viewfinder. At first the screen seemed fuzzy, swaying from a slammed door. It burst with snapped chair legs, cracking against the walls.

Tremors of pounding footsteps shook the floor. A guttural moan. The pewter candlestick was flung through the window, showering the sill in a tinkling of glass. Pages that were sprawled across the table flew up, flapping like wings. The ceiling bulb spun in a wild halo.

Still he could only see a grey smudged figure. At the clanging of the warning bell, it changed. The vibrations shook the room, louder and clashingly louder.

Ben gasped as a presence moved ever closer to the camera lens. Nearer and clearer. He recoiled. At first, he noticed the wild hair flecked in jagged spears of glass, a crazed smile with crooked teeth. But the worst part, by far the worst was the monster's eyes. The narrowed malevolent grey slits, as sharp as splinters of ice. His own eyes.

Fishing in Troubled Waters

"A community is like a ship; everyone ought to be prepared to take the helm."

Henrik Ibsen

"The sincere friends of this world are as ship lights in the stormiest of nights."

Giotto di Bondone

"It is good fishing in troubled waters."

Proverb

Dawn rose in a bloodied mackerel coloured sky over Clovelly harbour. The cottages huddled together in clusters, flanked either side of a steep cobblestone hill and shouldering only a side view of the sea, as though afraid to stare into its mortiferous depths.

Inside a cottage tucked into the bottom of the hill, Edna tied fish hooks on to thin lines with cracked, red hands. Her coarse brown skirts were runched up around her legs. She glanced at Peter's boots by the door, ready for him to be away with the tide. As the thud of his footfall on the stairs ceased, she looked towards him with dark, beseeching eyes. "Will you be taking Rufus with you this time?"

He roughly shook his head. "You know we don't take men on the boats when they've been drinking."

"Yes, I know Peter," her face looked gaunt and shadowy in the silvery light, "but Rufus is often found drinking. Without his catch the family will surely starve."

Peter looked away. "He should know better than to waste it all on porter!"

"But Mary has those bairns to feed and another on its way."

He rammed a foot into a boot. "She chose him. She should never have married that man!"

Edna lowered her voice, "He's new to these parts, not one of our own. Mary mistook a fish eye for a pearl."

Peter raked his hands through his dishevelled black hair. "We never take him when he's like this. He's a danger to the men, and the boat."

Edna thought of Mary's stooped, shivering body, the dark furrows gathering in puckers across her young face. Her shrieks carried in the wind and mingled with the screams of the gulls and the crashing of the waves. "You heard him shouting in the night Peter. She needs time to recover. Mary's screams chill my bones, for one day he will knock her stone dead."

"No good will come from this! He'll be an ill omen aboard the boat!" Peter slammed shut the wooden door.

For a moment she stared at it, to settle her breathing, before rising to continue her work.

Edna fastened the crayfish baskets, clambering over rocks and securing them in nooks and crannies. She patted Mary's shoulder as they worked side by side, her baby strapped around her middle. Edna glanced across and saw the beginning of a purplish black mark across her jaw line, before even the previous yellowish blur had time to fade. It could not be hidden by the limp, pale hair that circled around her face. They exchanged a meaningful look.

"You know he's been on the porter…" asked Mary.

Edna nodded. "It will give you a little peace, a chance to heal. If he returns, he should be sober for a few days."

"If?" Mary sighed. "But the danger to the men. Rufus has a terrible temper when he's been drinking. Peter's right to only take sober men on the boat; the risks are high enough already! There's a storm brewing and none of the fishermen can swim…"

Neither of them spoke, as they watched the fishing boat which bobbed impatiently for the seven men to clamber aboard. Flurries of foam flipped up the side of the wooden hull. An albatross circled and swooped low, giving a shrill cry.

On the quay side, facing the sea, the women spread out in front of trestle tables spread with gleaming piles of herrings. Against the thrashing of the waves was the flashing of sharp blades, slicing the silver fish sideways and slapping them down.

As evening fell, Edna took a lantern up to the cliff top to look out across the Ocean. The clouds bunched up into a brooding, bruised sky. Waves reared up and smashed against the intransigent cliffs, the spray flicking like spittle.

Edna recalled the time that she saw Rufus meandering along the cliff path and how she had hastily swung around and retreated in a different direction, eager to escape his florid face and burnished beard, which was always bristling with anger.

Darkness dropped quickly as she scrambled down the scree, shooting pebbles out from beneath her feet. It was a night without a moon, the sea lost in its own inky depths. She shuddered and drew her cloak around her.

The cottage shutters clattered in the increasing south-westerly wind, which wound its way down the chimney, whistling, whining and ululating. A chill crept around the room as she tossed on her straw mattress. Flickering behind her eyelids Edna thought of Peter. Would six fishermen be enough to restrain Rufus' temper? Had she placed an ill-omened curse upon the vessel? It was true; none of the men could swim. She thought of the slippery deck, the vertical drop and dive of the waves which thrashed the boat about.

Her sleep became battered and broken by the sound of the thunderous sea, creaking timbers and a sound like a

155

distant wailing. Even the cottage seemed to shudder and groan as she moaned in her sleep.

Dawn broke strangely calm, as though the sea had spent all of its fury. Edna scrunched along the shingle beach strewn with driftwood, as a pale, watery yellow sun seeped into the sky.

She held her breath as she scanned the horizon. It was bare, with no trace of a boat. Nothing. Just the keening and susurration of the waves.

Shadowy silhouettes of the wives left their cottages on the hill and stood looking across the sea. Like wraiths they fanned out and drifted in formation across the beach, to mend the nets in watchful silence. The women knew well the pattern of the tides, the vagaries of the weather and the hidden dangers concealed in coves or needle ended rocks jutting out along the coast line.

As a veil drew over the long day, Edna made a broth for her supper. She curled herself by the hearth, seeking comfort in the lapping flames.

Some sound must have awoken her, for she sat up rigidly in her chair. A log had capsized onto the flagstone floor where it lay, hissing and sizzling.

Then she heard it again, she was certain. Her heart thumped as she wrapped her shawl around her shoulders and heaved the wooden door open. Edna turned towards the bay and gasped. Buffeted by the waves, she saw the moored fishing vessel, its limp sails curled languidly in the bow.

So where was Peter? She swung around and looked upwards. Only six stooped figures staggered up the hill as though they had lead in their boots.

Edna clung to her door frame as each figure peeled off into one of the houses, until she was standing alone. Solitary as a post. Frozen.

If she hadn't entreated Peter to take Rufus, he might be

returning to her hearth. Now she had lost everything. A deep hollowness gnawed inside her.

Then she saw the door of Mary's cottage open and a man stepped out. Like a sleepwalker he drifted back down the hill. "I had to tell her!" he called out. "We lost him around Morte Point. I couldn't let her and the bairns keep waiting, without knowing that we would provide for them."

Edna looked up into his salt-encrusted cracked skin, which had lined into hard ridges. He had returned. For this night at least, he was safe from the sea. Her knees collapsed beneath her and she sat on the cold stone step.

In a distant field she heard the shriek of a fox.

Fishing in Troubled Waters was selected as one of the winners in the Waterloo Festival short story competition, "Transforming Communities", and published in Transformations in December 2020.

Like to Read More Work Like This?

Then sign up to our mailing list and download our free collection of short stories, *Magnetism*. Sign up now to receive this free e-book and also to find out about all of our new publications and offers.

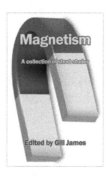

Sign up here:
  http://eepurl.com/gbpdVz

Please Leave a Review

Reviews are so important to writers. Please take the time to review this book. A couple of lines is fine.

Reviews help the book to become more visible to buyers. Retailers will promote books with multiple reviews.

This in turn helps us to sell more books… And then we can afford to publish more books like this one.

Leaving a review is very easy.

Go to https://bit.ly/3IIx8Y5, scroll down the left-hand side of the Amazon page and click on the "Write a customer review" button.

Other Writing by Linda Flynn

A Most Amazing Zoo

Illustrated by Linda Laurie

What happens when the Queen visits Zedgate Zoo? Well she meets a lot of amazing animals and finds out a lot of amazing facts about them.

This delightful story is told through a series of colourful and entertaining pictures and a lively text. There is plenty of extra story in the pictures for the child who has the book read to them, and the text is of an appropriate language level for the emergent reader.

"This is a beautifully presented book and the story is both fun and packed with facts. The illustrations are amazing, the animals' characters shine through and there's lots of fine detail and humour." *(Amazon)*

Order from Amazon:

Paperback: ISBN 978-1-910542-48-4

Chapeltown Books

Linda's stories have appeared in the following Bridge House and Chapeltown Books anthologies:

   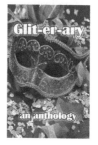

  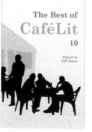 

Other Publications by Bridge House

Fresh Beginnings

by Leela Dutt
illustrated by Kate Attfield

An intriguing mixture of stories, all in Leela Dutt's inimitable style – something here for everyone, and beautifully illustrated by Kate Attfield.

Some are short and funny, some poignant – Leela Dutt's collection *Fresh Beginnings* will warm your heart and stay in your mind – it might even make you laugh!

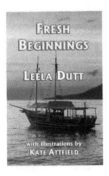

"If you like short stories, if you like good stories, then *Fresh Beginnings* is for you." (*Amazon*)

Order from Amazon:

Paperback: ISBN 978-1-914199-12-7
eBook: ISBN 978-1-914199-13-4

What If...

by Anne Wilson

"What if?" An unanswered question. The unexplained, a mystery, a road not taken. This is a collection of dark fiction injected here and there with glimmers of humour.

The author takes us on a surreal and ghostly journey from Latin America's Day of the Dead, through the coastal towns of Lancashire, a pig farm in Denmark, a high-rise in Mallorca, a haunted vicarage at Christmas and a town centre coffee bar. The voices we hear are variously plaintive, nostalgic, and occasionally vindictive or vengeful: the testimonies and fears of the living and the dead.

"The author weaves a thrilling web with her prose, creating delightful pocket worlds to entice and entrance the reader. These are stories that linger long in the mind after reading." (*Amazon*)

Order from Amazon:

Paperback: ISBN: 978-1-914199-14-1
eBook: 978-1-914199-15-8

The Memory Keeper

by S. Nadja Zajdman

In these eighteen linked stories, the reader accompanies our
heroine Noela ("born on Santa Clause's Day!") as she develops
from an insecure Daddy's Girl into a woman willing and able
to stand on her own. Go on this journey with her as she meets
challenge after challenge and as her relationships with all
around her change.

The Memory Keeper is a collection of tales about a life well
learnt in S. Nadja Zajdman's distinctive story-teller voice.

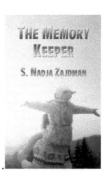

"A really lovely collection –I'm going to read mine again."
(Amazon)

Order from Amazon:

Paperback: ISBN: 978-1-914199-18-9
eBook: 978-1-914199-19-6

Lightning Source UK Ltd.
Milton Keynes UK
UKHW021323221222
414331UK00021B/604